LUMINOUS FISH

LUMINOUS FISH

Tales of Science and Love

LYNN MARGULIS

A Sciencewriters Book

CHELSEA GREEN PUBLISHING COMPANY
White River Junction, Vermont

The photo of *Photoblepharon palpebratus* accompanying the Prologue and Epilogue is
reproduced by permission of John E. Randall. All rights reserved.

Copy Editor: Judith Herrick Beard
Proofreader: Jim Wallace
Designer: Peter Holm, Sterling Hill Productions
Design Assistant: Daria Hoak, Sterling Hill Productions
Cover Design: Kimberly Glyder, Kimberly Glyder Design

Printed in the United States
First printing, January 2007
10 9 8 7 6 5 4 3 2 1

Originally published as *Peces Luminosos: Historias de Amor y Ciencia* by Tusquets
Editorial, Barcelona, 2002.

Our Commitment to Green Publishing
Chelsea Green sees publishing as a tool for cultural change and ecological steward-
ship. We strive to align our book manufacturing practices with our editorial mission,
and to reduce the impact of our business enterprise on the environment. We print our
books and catalogs on chlorine-free recycled paper, using soy-based inks, whenever
possible. This book may cost slightly more because we use recycled paper, and we
hope you'll agree that it's worth it. Chelsea Green is a member of the Green Press
Initiative (www.greenpressinitiative.org), a nonprofit coalition of publishers, manufacturers, and authors working to protect the world's endangered forests and con-
serve natural resources.
    Luminous Fish was printed on Natures Natural, a 50 percent post–consumer
waste recycled paper supplied by Thomson-Shore.

Library of Congress Cataloging-in-Publication Data
Margulis, Lynn, 1938-
  Luminous fish : tales of science and love / Lynn Margulis.
     p. cm.
  "Sciencewriters Books."
  Stories, fictional and memoir, of scientists in work and in love.
  ISBN-13: 978-1-933392-33-2
  ISBN-10: 1-933392-33-9
  1. Scientists—Fiction. I. Title.

  PS3613.A745L86 2007
  813'.6—dc22   2006025902

A Sciencewriters Book

scientific knowledge through enchantment
Sciencewriters Books is an imprint of Chelsea Green Publishing. Founded and codirected
by Lynn Margulis and Dorion Sagan, Sciencewriters is an educational partnership
devoted to advancing science through enchantment in the form of the finest possible
books, videos, and other media.

Chelsea Green Publishing Company
Post Office Box 428
White River Junction, Vermont 05001
(800) 639-4099 | www.chelseagreen.com

FOR
Jennifer Margulis di Properzio,
James di Properzio,
Hesperus, Athena, and Etani.

CONTENTS

PROLOGUE

Photoblepharon

A genus of teleost (bony) fish in the family Anomalopidae (nocturnal flashlight fishes) found principally in the reef habitats of the Indo-West Pacific ocean. They bear paired organs beneath the eyes that harbor luminous bacterial symbionts. The light produced by the bacteria is used in mating, foraging, and predator avoidance behavior. In captivity the bacterial symbionts are often lost and therefore the fish is rendered incapable of all behaviors that require underwater light.

These flashlight fish cause the patchy light in the luminous bay off Eilat, Israel. Except for men in boats on assignment from the New England and Monaco Royal aquaria, the night fishermen avoid them. The bright lights bob and submerge as schools course through the moonlit water. Like women no longer lovers, the cold lights extinguish after some months at home in captivity. Once dazzling, the aquarium flashlight fish now resemble garbage carp.

Each fish eerily glows in the dark as it shines on potential prey. The cold light, enough to expose a sheet of film, radiates in the sediments. In pockets in their guts live crowds of bacteria. The bacterial symbionts, luminous without cessation, know only to glow. Each fish "baffles"—it exposes and then hides its radiant tissue, imposing its will on the steady light of its myriad tiny captives. How did this ideal partnership evolve? Why do fish sport silvery mirrors that reflect light generated by packed bacteria? Because bacterial-ridden ancestral fish survived to leave more offspring than their less happily infected relatives. Those with silvery bellysides and eyes that glowed with luminous bacteria are less visible to their attackers from below. Potential predators see no fish. They think they see to the lit surface above the water, the sky. The marine scientists call such camouflage "counter-illumination."

The story of science, a continuous joint narrative, is never the personal tale of any scientist. In the proximity of flash-light fish, local scenes dazzle brightly and disappear. This kind of strong illumination dispels for a moment scientific darkness and anonymity. Howard's medical machinations, René's wilfulness, Raoul's balloons prior to the start of the freon-ozone war, and Georges's love affairs impact calculations, flash, and then fade. Science theorizes the general but studies the peculiar, the particular, the arcane, and the idio-syncratic. Scientists suppress their urges as they coax and cajole the natural world to yield her secrets. Here I describe the social and sexual distractions, the passion suppression, the particular weirdness, a sample of the very few men and women who devote their lives to science.

. . . permit me to tell you [Mosser, her lover, to Emma, the wife of Max von Forschung, Professor Ordinarius at the University of Wurzburg, Geheimrath] that men bottled up in scientific investigations never love anything but science. Given the choice between a beauty and a microbe, they opt for the latter. For them, a woman represents—at the most—a fleeting, disturbing episode that occurred in their youth.

Santiago Ramón y Cajal (1852–1934) *Vacation Stories*, p. 18, translated by Laura Otis, University of Illinois Press, Urbana, 2001

CONCEITS
(Howard)

Our feelings lead us at first to believe that absolute truth must lie within our realm, but study takes from us, little by little, these chimerical conceits.

Claude Bernard, 1813–1878
"An Introduction to the Study of Experimental Medicine," p. 121 in *The Nature of Life, Readings in Biology*, The Great Books Foundation, Chicago, 2001

It begins in the spring, when all such things begin, even among the parts of a single flower. Malaise, sense of responsibility—never ambition—carries him after supper back to the library to the neck-open cadavers of the anatomy lab. Twice a week or so, he joins his cronies at Jimmy's Tavern. The white ride cards—most of them offer to share expenses to New York City during spring break—festoon the damp walls. *Chicago Sun Times* editorials and leftist political cartoons make it easy to seem as if one is reading. Howard assesses the availability of each young woman who enters the barroom. A poor reproduction of Botticelli's Birth of Venus, the voluptuous virgin emerging from the modest shell, hangs next to a picture of the skinny young men of the University of Chicago varsity basketball team. Behind them is Jimmy, the owner and bartender.

The mere presence of Howard Fein amuses his former dorm dwellers, Andrew (Andy) Carelli and Richie Baum. Richie, as usual, is obsessed with Howard, and restless. Awed by Carelli—the ham radio operator and Proust reader from Waco, Texas—he smirks at Howard.

"Richie, go find me a spring vacation ride to New York. The City, of course." Howard orders another pitcher as he pours beers for his friends; nothing for himself. Richie mumbles as he scans the cards. Returning, he throws a soiled index card on the round wooden table.

"Look at this," Richie says. "The guy writing this one's a fool. He's self-effacing. You don't want to go anywhere with him." He reads it aloud: "'Wanted: a ride to Hawley-Wallenpawpack Pennsylvania (Scranton) over spring vacation. can drive, willing to share expenses. call Dorchester 4-4789.' See the false modesty, all the absent I's and his use of the lower case? I should be a fortune-teller." Richie drops another card faceup on the table, amused. Carelli turns his freckled face, irritated at Richie's smugness. "'Wanted: Grad student to share apartment near campus with amiable male. Quiet studious. Likes good music.' This guy's phony. Probably a fairy pick-up invite. Has to impress the world that he's cultured, but lacks self-confidence. He's trying to compensate by conspicuous assertions." Richie flips the card in the general direction of Carelli's head.

Howard ignores him. "Carelli," he continues in a soft, almost caressing voice, "I'll figure out my own ride. You tell Richie in front of me again what you mean by the 'verifiability principle.'"

Carelli begins his answer as Howard's attention drifts and

then fixes on the young woman squinting at the front door. He sips his pop as he watches her: her shoulder-strap bag, her sandals, her long dark hair and even-featured face. She comes into the subdued light where the men see her far more clearly than she sees anything. She stands awkwardly. She hesitates, but Richie catches her eye, motions to her, and she walks over.

"Organization, Methods and Principles of Knowledge?" she asks Richie. She ducks toward the single empty seat at the men's table. She sits down far less conspicuously than she wishes as one of her chair legs catches squeekily.

"Yeah, I know you—it's me, we're both in OMP—Prof. Eberhardt's section." Richie imagines her in bed. He kicks her chair lightly. "René, right?" She nods. "Pay no attention to them." His left hand dismisses Howard and Andy as he stage-whispers to her behind his other hand.

Even though she slipped in right next to him, Howard ignores the girl. He is singularly focused on Carelli as he props his hiking boots on the edge of Carelli's chair. "Your 'verifiability principle' says a general statement is true as long as all of its consequences can be verified by observation and data. Any statement not borne out by the facts must be revised. Right? But I say any statement is one of two things: either a tautology or an empirical observation."

Hunched in concentration, Carelli answers, "Yes, but that doesn't mean the verifiability principle is definitional and therefore meaningless."

With a scowl, Richie asserts, "Mmm, meaningless!" and nods to the girl. "Hey, Jimmy," he calls out. "We ordered another pitcher, but this hasn't been 'borne out by the facts.'"

Howard peers at Carelli: "Well, if it's empirical, you have to find some fact to contradict it. If I claim, say, that gravity accelerates things toward the center of the Earth and inductively verify it by a lot of examples . . . and then if I predict the acceleration, you accept it as 'Truth,' at least until I show you a counterexample. Like something falling up. That is, something falling up would contradict the tentative, but verifiable, law of gravity that tentatively we have accepted." Lingering over each of his self-consciously chosen words, Howard is radiant. He glances at the girl but does not betray his notice of how exciting and attractive she looks. Wow, how young. And then he recognizes her. Nothing to do with the likelihood that she attends Richie's philosophy class taught by Professor Eberhardt. Howard had gazed at her once before, also in an ill-lit place. But not here in this—or any other—bar. He masks the shock of recognition by avoiding her glance; he drops his eyes under half-closed lids. "What evidence could contradict the 'verifiability principle' itself?" he asks Carelli as his index finger draws slow circles in the table's puddle of spilt beer. "I tell you, smart-ass Andy Carelli, that nothing could. The 'verifiability principle' is definitional, not empirical, and therefore *unfalsifiable*." Howard pauses, looks around, proud of himself.

The girl, annoyed, frowns. She stares at Howard, who reluctantly responds with a leer. She looks away. She blurts, "No, *you* have a fallacy there—his verifiability principle is no testable physical law, it's a different kind of statement, a sort of summary. I mean, it's a generalization that covers all kinds of physical laws, laws that are more than simple statements.

Basically it's a generalization. To deny it you need to examine any of the parts you may be concerned with at the time."

"Sure," Richie says. "She's right, Howie, it's generalization."

She continues, "It's like if I said 'physical laws govern the universe,' you wouldn't be able to think of specific contradictions. And my statement wouldn't be definitional either."

She is out of breath.

"This is René," says Richie, "she's in my class."

"Maybe you're right," Howard nods his head, ogling her. "René, huh? Well, nice to meet you. But I still ask myself if saying 'physical laws govern the universe' has any informational content. Isn't that, like the verifiability principle, just an arbitrary opinion, like 'art is beautiful'? The point is that there is simply no real way of proving or disproving it. Like everything." His tone is both conciliatory and condescending. She *was* the same woman he saw in the darkness. Her straight-nosed profile was laudable. In only his second act of voyeurism in his life, Howard had watched them, Samuel Guggenheim and her, behind the statue.

"It's obvious anyway to me," says the redheaded Carelli, lowering his voice intimately as if to restrain the escape of his southern accent, "that the only way we know anything at all is by observing it either directly or with some device. We observe something, try to generalize about it, and try to make predictions about the next one of that particular class of things to come around. We are empiricists. We believe in data, redemption and salvation, a clean soul, and a pure heart. I really felt left out when my little brother Timmy came up to me and told me that I can't know. He bawls out to everyone that I can't understand life or anything else because I'm in such bad shape—I doubt the existence of God. That runty pain-in-the-neck keeps claiming that I am already corrupt. My mother, brother, father are true believers. I used to be able to understand how they talk. I used to know what they meant. I remember—I must have talked just like Timmy does now."

He clucks his tongue. "Meanwhile, my sister's husband left her—four months ago. She's got three kids and they can't even locate him. I think he ran off with the nineteen-year-old babysitter. My parents don't even mention it. Timmy doesn't talk about them anymore either. It's like none of this even exists."

Howard cuts in: "The trouble is, Carelli, I'm not sure that you—that any of us—have the right to say the people who follow Jesus are wrong. What gives you or me any right to judge? I hesitate to tell you, or to tell anyone else for that matter—especially in this company—what they ought to believe. *I* wouldn't tell your little brother that to still obsess over the execution of a bearded, kindly thirty-three-year-old Jew from twenty centuries ago is crazy. Maybe we don't see everything there is to see. At least your brother feels something. At least he realizes suffering and knows just exactly what it is that he's supposed to do. Most people have a great way of avoiding and evading. They shut it all out. People all over have slid into massive, inert indifference. Look at Nazi Germany."

"You're so right: people don't see anything," René agrees. She tries to wrest away his attention as she leans forward and looks intensely at Howard. She blushes as Howard returns her gaze, equally intently. He knows for sure that she doesn't recognize him. He was hidden in the shadows that night. She looked the same then as she does now, only more excited, wiggly, and breathless as Guggenheim reached up her skirt for a fast feel. Guggenheim, Samuel Carter A. Guggenheim, is the "house head" at Burton-Judson. An Upper Manhattanite, he refers to his bathrobe as a "dressing gown" and requests the men call him "Mr. Guggenheim," even in the lavatory. Guggenheim crosses his sevens, a habit he claimed he learned from Europeans during annual Alpine ski trips. "Crossed sevens are the norm of astronomical notation," Howard overheard him say to a puny bespectacled science major. Guggenheim always calls the twenty-sixth letter of the alphabet "zed." He is obsessed with the seduction of young women.

Guggenheim had introduced Howard to kumquats. Howard pretended to know them. He betrayed his lack of acquaintance when he bit into one and grimaced at its tartness. This same Samuel Guggenheim had initiated some rather famous provocative and bisexual incidents. His reputation of acts of dubious propriety for a dorm director was the envy of undergraduate residents. Nobody knew what really happened but the story about the Guggenheim action that had begun in writing was especially plausible. Unsigned, explicit, and suspiciously similar notes written in left-slanted script, the word was, had been passed to at least three people. Each was addressed as the object of romantic and erotic longing. The gossip reached Howard during a scheduled early evening showing of Truffaut's *Les 400 Coups* on the second floor of Ida Noyes Hall. A note later appeared taped to the dorm clothes dryer (near the "hold-for-10-seconds" button). Other nearly identical copies served as gum wrappers—at least five—passed around in the dimly lit makeshift movie hall. The one Howard intercepted and could personally vouch for read:

> Dun-colored beauty,
> Come to me tonight. I need to know
> if the blond straightness of your flowing locks rivals
> your shorter hairs, presumptive curls of below.
> You must stand mutely while I explore,
> descending.

Another set of incidents was a sequence of trysts among and behind certain giant sculptures. Richie had told Howard that Guggenheim had felt up at least two students—one of each gender—and in public. He described these trysts with so much detail that Howard began to feel left out. Richie knew so much about Guggenheim's exploits that it was hard not to wonder. Richie said that Guggenheim had style: he placed his left hand discretely on the young man's zipper while discoursing to him at the downtown museum. The boy was too mortified to move, afraid to cause a scene. When Guggenheim ceased both his lecture and his ministrations, the embarrassed, excited student glanced at him, then looked back at the display and said, shyly, "Shall we continue?"

Two days later, without interrupting his own monologue on Southeast Asian religion, he had, after lifting her skirt, inserted his warm fingers into a Far Eastern studies major. Curiously, both incidents occurred against the glass cases of

Khmer colossal heads from ancient Cambodia at the Art Institute of Chicago. Howard wondered if Guggenheim enjoyed some arcane connection to Cambodia. Dennis O'Donahue, the most handsome and banal person in Burton-Judson, was also rumored to have been one of Guggenheim's casual conquests. O'Donahue was such a straight B+ try-hard with such an athlete's body that Howard suspected Guggenheim started the rumor himself.

Howard directly witnessed one Guggenheim peccadillo. The projector had been manned by Guggenheim at another Cocteau showing (*La Belle et la Bête*) the last Wednesday in February. At the back of the hall, behind the final unoccupied rows of seats, Guggenheim brought in and gently seated, his two hands on her shoulders, an ingénue. He explained in earnest terms his attempt to bring culture to his semiliterate mid-Western colleagues. Howard, unenthused about the Cocteau film but too bored that night not to check it out, had tardily slipped in quietly by the back door. At that moment Howard was the only person in the hall who saw the silhouettes of Guggenheim and the girl, who stood together behind the projector. As Guggenheim knelt to point out the complexity of operations she would need to shut off the projector, he beckoned to his svelte companion as she bent over the machine. Howard actually saw him slowly insert his hand and raise it under her short skirt. Howard, on this his first voyeurism experience, ducked into the shadows. But he did creep forward for a better view. She abruptly stood partway up, checked about, then settled her hands back on her knees and arched her back. Howard found himself fascinated by Guggenheim's techniques.

Watching them brought to mind how awkward he had been with Janey, his first girl. The fumbling, self-conscious hesitations; his high expectations; working all too quickly to a disappointing end that released her as well, with surprising flatulence. He never quite brought himself even to date Janey again, let alone seduce her. Guggenheim's admirable style insured complicity while it precluded distracting conversation. His mode nagged at Howard. As he watched them he told himself that Mr. Guggenheim's inimitable talents were for actions less than honorable. Howard himself could never lead on any woman or girl this way, and the idea of caressing an erect penis sickened him. Howard's decision to stay away from anyone who might become too engaged was utterly conscious. Women fell in love with him too easily.

"Everyone needs his fantasies," Carelli's voice breaks through his musings. Howard jump-starts. He's been staring absently at René. Carelli speaks clearly, with little trace of his southern drawl.

"We need our dreams. It's not just that we need our sleep. That research by Schizer in which they deprived people of their dreaming; remember? They woke their subjects up as soon as—well, they shook the subjects just as their eyelids began to twitch. The 'control' group were those deprived of sleep. But the 'controls' were permitted normal dream time. They did dream; no deprivation. Those people who were not allowed to dream started to worry. All of them became neurotic and depressed. Those who were only deprived of sleep weren't at all affected, they showed no symptoms. See, I think I'm right; I believe there must be some scientific law, some rule of conservation of fantasy. If you see it my way, you'll see this Jesus stuff is just an example, a viable fantasy. We all need a given quantity of dreaming, of fantasy. Always. Daily. We supposed intellectuals individualize our fantasies a little more. We see ourselves as subtle and more original. You know what? I think my way of explaining Schizer's results as 'conservation of fantasy' is an original idea. I think I'll write it up."

Howard pours more beer for everyone except himself. "Do you always have to quantify everything, Andy?" he says. Carelli doesn't respond; his silence as usual unnerves Howard. They all become quiet, Carelli, Richie, and René sucking down beer. Richie looks at René. Howard looks at his soda. Carelli is so enviable—he always sees everything clearly. Howard considers Andy Carelli to be the most mentally tidy person he knows. Once on a very warm spring night Andy walked into their shared dorm room to grab his towel at 3 a.m. and unwittingly witnessed Howard masturbating. Carelli only smiled. He never gossiped. He rarely acknowledges anything. His mere presence heightened Howard's insecurity. He seems to know so much that Howard does not, deep truths about everything, about life. But mostly Howard feels Carelli knows about him. Often Howard thinks Carelli is the only person who really knows him.

Howard stands up, drops three dollars on the table (less than what he owes), and grabs René's hand in an unabashed move—he has been inspired by Guggenheim musings. She does not object. He savors her secret victimization by Guggenheim. Then he drops her hand and walks briskly out of Jimmy's door. Suddenly he begins to wonder about Leon Bloom's class—the practical anatomy quiz scheduled for the morning. Oh, damn—it already is morning. Amused, he internally compliments himself on his hand-grab technique; he knows that she is already in love with him.

Only two weeks later, after René tells him that she has accepted a summer research job—for all three months—does he even suggest they meet. They speak on the phone, routinely after Jimmy's, nearly every night. René obtained Howard's phone number from Richie; Howard, who replaces Schubert with Mahler music in the background, modulates the phonograph with the hand not holding the telephone. He considers all conversations with René amusing breaks from his studies.

He tells her about his Bronx childhood, how inspired he was—and still is—to engage in "real work," farm work. He adores backpacking, the edge of danger. His interest in theosophy probably compensates for his lapsed Jewish education.

"I answered an ad in the *New York Times* one Christmas, for inexpensive firewood. Once there, upstate, way upstate, I liked it so much that I convinced the farmer to give me a summer job."

"You wanted to live on a farm?" René seems surprised. "I avoid your 'real work.' I always dreamed about coming to the city."

"How weird," Howard scratches the record as he relieves Mahler and introduces Mozart, "that you lived where I wanted to be. I grew up in a small, immaculate brownstone apartment with a fireplace. I went home for holidays and started choking. My parents thought I was crazy."

Howard remembers the farm summer vividly: a landscape, unobstructed by people, unsullied by the filthy or elegant multitudes of New York. To load the wood in his father's Oldsmobile, to drive by himself to Larsen's, to do the real work. Newly fallen snow lay against the brown of oaks unwilling to part with their leaves until late spring. White prevailed against red dabs, the caps of children sledding on the mountain slopes. The stash of wood he began by himself to remove from an enormous pile. He was grateful for the chance. At Larsen's command, the hired man helped Howard tie logs onto the luggage rack after he had loaded them into the trunk, back seat, floor, and front seat. Twigs and bits of sawdust sullied the plush blue upholstery of his father's car. Howard's arms grew weary, his palms scratched, with little bloody cuts. The farm sat on the crest of a hill; a kingdom of trees, animals, and shrubs looking down into the valley. A few weeks later, after two short letters were exchanged, Larsen hired Howard for the summer.

"My mother visited the farm," Howard tells René, his hand rising as the mock conductor of the musical crescendo. "She came by herself in her white Pontiac convertible. She looked so out of place. She felt vulnerable and lost. She meant well but she acted like a pain in the ass."

It had been a warm breezy morning in mid-July, redolent with a smell of happiness. The chicken house thermostat was acting up and there were dozens of the furry little idiots hatching that week. Nobler were the trees, birch, oak, and a row of tall hemlocks. Before his mother's arrival, Howard watched a barn swallow swoop and disappear under an overhanging roof ledge of the cabin. A cottontail came from nowhere and looked at him, twitched her nose coquettishly and dashed off. The day before, the twin Larsen boys had found her babies, snug in their camouflaged hole.

Mrs. Fein had left the car roof in place to avoid mussing her hair. The first thing she said when she saw him was, "My God, how do you live in this mess? . . . No signs at all, as though everyone was expected to know that this paved road was rural route 4A. I'm lucky I made it, no wonder I'm late!" She kissed the air by his cheek in greeting and rumpled his hair. She looked at him displeased. "For God's sake, it wouldn't hurt you at all if you did a little washing! What would your father say?"

They had gone into his cabin. Chattering to Howard, Mrs. Fein set herself to sifting and sorting his dirty laundry. She made him remove his socks so she could wash them. "I just hate to see you living like this, that's all, dear," she said in a kinder tone. She pinned back a few scattered hairs and wiped her forehead. Her hair was grayer than Howard had remembered. She was still so pretty, he liked looking at her. But as he pulled off his socks he felt a familiar, humiliating sense of shame.

"Your father works too hard," his mother was saying. "The shop gets him down. After all these years. It makes me sick how he pushes himself. There just is no one. No one he can trust with the work. There is no one like him left. No one who works like that anymore. Someone must succeed him, but there isn't anybody. The Puerto Ricans are worse than the Negroes. And this spring he took the usual beating from the union. He didn't eat anything for two weeks. He takes it all so personally, and, really, sometimes I think he thinks more of the workers than of himself."

She examined the unflaked polish of her fingernails.

"You weighed much more when you left home. Frankly, I don't think you look well at all."

"I weigh plenty, I feel fine, and I like it here, Mom." He could tell his voice was too high pitched.

"Well, you'll probably stay a slob. I'm afraid I always did too much for you—all the time—it's probably too late now."

He tells René that he still wants to conduct music. He doesn't worry about neatness. When his parents listened to classical music, he would come into their room, stand by the foot of the bed, and wave his hands wildly, only slightly out of time. Howard recalls to René that his father carried the weight of the world on his shoulders, and his mother, when she wasn't smiling and preening herself for others, held her mouth in a disapproving frown that was as often a display for Howard and his sister and brother as for his father. Howard idealizes his parents. Medical school for Howard, or his brother, is now and always has been his father's dream. The day he told them he'd been accepted, his mother sent him three weeks early, a chocolate birthday cake and candles from Rosenfeld's.

René says she grew up in upper Canada, where Roger Pemberlain, her father, was a better field geologist than his citified boss. Her mother tried in vain to keep their home in some semblance of her own lace-curtain upbringing. René's father, a strong handsome miner, watched the Sudbury iron being stripped away. He chafed and brooded over what he could not fix: a boss beholden to the moneyed interests, the felling of trees. Brown and red iron-ore rocks traveled down the river to the great lake for eventual conversion to Gary, Indiana, steel and Detroit, Michigan, cars. René tells Howard that her father was instantly distinguishable from his rough-hewn coworkers by a single fact: he was devoted to books.

Without listening very carefully to her measured speech Howard learns that René yearned for the city, for bookstores, for intellectual men. She wanted time to read. She hopes never to have to return to Schreiber Beach, Ontario, at least in the winter. She loves books. She still shares poetry and novels with her father. She finds, as a good student, that there is nothing left but to go on. How educated her fellow University of Chicago students seem, doesn't Howard think so too? She guesses she excels at both field and written work, but, she tells him, she still is awed by the culture Chicago offers and is always amazed by the wit, the erudition of their fellow students.

All of this by phone until finally Howard relents. He agrees to sacrifice time in his frenetic schedule to meet her in the flesh. René arrives early at the meeting place, a secondhand bookstore at Fifty-fifth and Woodlawn, "Pages." She looks aimlessly at the books on the bargain table and watches the cars.

The sky is dark when Howard, nearly a full hour late and not even alone, finally pulls up in his antiquated green Chevy. Richie Baum—even more the buffoon—sits in the front seat. René eyes him for an instant, crestfallen. She screws her face into a false smile. "Hi, Richie," she says, unable to suppress her disappointment.

Howard calls, "Hey, René, don't just stand there, get in. I'm just going to drop Richie off at Jimmy's."

"Sure," she grins, masking her relief.

"We were just talking about people's stupid ideas about others, parents' expectations, what you can really know about somebody. I don't know, Richie; all those things my parents think about me—I'm still trying to un-learn about *myself*."

Richie says in a singsong voice, "A man's character is his fate. That's what Heraclitus wrote. Hey, here it is." Howard stops and idles. Richie climbs out with a backhand wave.

When she gets in the front seat, Howard pats her leg with a patronizing lack of apology.

"Do you know where I shall take you now?" He grins.

"No."

"You'll see," he mutters with supreme and sexy confidence.

"Palos Park," says the sign. She contains her excitement. 'To bed' is what she had *wanted* to answer. "Palos Park has the only hills outcropping for hundreds of square miles of prairie. Glacial moraines, trees, damp scent. I want to show you last year's leaves and this year's rivulets. I think 'palos' means 'sticks' in Spanish."

Howard contemplates the burdens of southbound traffic they will inevitably have to suffer upon return. But he smiles, seduction mode, at René. Maybe they would find a private place in the park. Maybe they would have enough time.

They didn't. The luxury of Palos Park greenery became a memory of bumper-to-bumper frustration. He should have known.

On the second date, Howard grabs her hand and makes her run. They dash together, bound past the parked cars. René's skirt rubs against her shins. He pulls her beyond the greenness of the lawn, its matted grass, and *Typha*-tasseled wet edges. The trees here are in such dense stands that, barring the *Ailanthus* groves, they cannot see that Jackson Park and the Midway are just beyond. The Museum of Science and Industry, the Aquarium, The Loop and all the rest, the waterfront and pumping station are temporarily hidden in the natural hideaway.

Breathing heavily, the adult children find themselves in the exact center of the secret Round Garden. Not a soul can be seen; four million are hidden by shrubbery and overgrowth. All of them are barred from the moist nature by ignorance of this hidden, sacred site. The garden at dusk is theirs alone. Directly east, the unpeopled thicket is not only very green but its dampness provokes his sweat, stimulates her wetness. Crepuscular forms, nonhuman, forage in the humid stillness. An owl hoots. The light reveals scurrying unknowables. They enjoy their tightly clasped hands. They move tentatively into the shadowy grove. The moon rises silent in the east, inviolate. Shadow patterns shift. Another hoot, some squawks, rustles. A leaf falls where a nuthatch flutters. Darkness goads the waxing moon, encompassed by selenocentric rings.

René remembers this for the rest of her life; the first time, and, she surmises, it will be the last time she is in love. She yields easily as Howard pulls her down. He is no burden to her, underneath him on the grass. She is suffused by his body's warmth. He kisses her neck, her arms, her lips. He recalls to himself the night he watched her in the shadows; memories of Guggenheim agitate him. He feels the urgency of possession. He relishes the rare moment of knowledge of exactly what he wants. Desire, a foreign passion, rises within him. While she lingers in the warmth and the wild, he burrows purposefully under her skirt.

"You shouldn't be so emotionally involved, especially with me," he murmurs to her afterward, "I really like you a lot but together we aren't important. Please, René, I don't want you to get hurt." He takes her hand, bends down each finger in turn. She is startled, and looks so innocent, so bewildered, so abandoned. He is instantly sorry that he has actually verbalized this habitual response, this kneejerk reluctance. Again he cannot help the unilateralness. That young women find him sexy is the burden of his dispassionate tentative being. "Let's go back now, right now. I left a leg—no, not really; a knee, shin, ankle, and foot—in formaldehyde," Howard says, as he buttons his shirt. René still sits on the damp ground, moongazing. He actually pats her on the head again. "I really like you a lot."

Howard lies on the bed listening to Shostakovitch's Fifth Symphony. This morning it is still dark inside the Sixty-second Street apartment. Outside the clouds obscure the setting moon, if any. The usual mess abounds in the small student ghetto apartment: tattered menus, postcard art reproductions, anatomy and pharmacology textbooks open to various pages or piled on the dusty shelf. Outside: irate honking, a comforting tedium of automobiles. Bicycle bells tinkling, their brakes yearning for oil. The secretary next door leaves for work late. She slams and double-locks her door in sexual and professional frustration. A quick clatter of dishes testifies that some still eat at home. The El screeches.

Then the gradual cessation of the elevated train's clang gives way to halt. The phone rings. He jumps up to answer. He switches on the reading lamp. He can hardly hear René's voice at the other end of the line. He picks up his darts. Schmidt, that gets him for lowering my grade, dead center. And Professor Porter-Smith . . . And Mother . . . He hits the homemade yellow bull's eye three times while not listening to her.

"What?" Suddenly Howard pays attention. Now the telephone voice is melodious, and the message unmistakable.

"I missed my period so I went for a rabbit test last week. The results just came. With the bill." A long silence follows, both Howard and René feel their respective hearts beat and listen to the telephone static.

"What am I supposed to say?" he finally asks, breaking the silence. But then, as if ashamed of his callousness, his voice takes on a gentleness. "Do you want me to apologize? Or maybe . . ."

"Or maybe what?"

"Or maybe you just want the truth."

"What truth? You claim there is no truth. Don't play games."

"Well, René," Howard says slowly, "well. . . maybe it will console you to know—for sure—that I felt absolutely perfect at the time. It was perfect for me. I never even feel good—let alone perfect. What more should I say?" He could hear her softly crying.

"It'll be OK, kid," he says gently. "Let's talk about it tomorrow. Schmidt's lab exam is this morning. I have a million things to do. We'll work it all out by tomorrow afternoon.

Believe me, trust me. This is just part of my promise to *try* to think ahead." The click of the receiver echoes in his head. He imagines her fertilized egg now, as it travels the length of her right fallopian tube and implants along her uterus. He recalls the woman's cadaver he dissected last year. But today it is his seed in that little egg. The new life would probably grow brown-eyed, black curly-haired, just like him. He imagines a little boy with high cheekbones and a nose that doesn't curve before adolescence. He hoists the kid onto the sink, keeps him at his side while he shaves in the morning. He tells stories to the black-haired son. He talks through the thick of the white lather on his face they both pretend is whipped cream. He tip-toes into the kitchen, so as not to wake up mommy. His little boy, from the vantage point of the counter, helps him pour milk into two separate unequal cereal bowls. Raisin bran. Lots of extra raisins for his son. He tells the kid that protein in milk and the iron in the raisins will help him grow to be as big and strong as daddy. And when some of the cereal spills on the floor, he does not yell at the boy—he will not act like his father. Both the kid and he ignore their mess. Smiling conspiratorily they leave the cleanup for mommy.

Then Howard goes off to the hospital. He can see it now. At night he returns to the cozy home. The nice home in the nice neighborhood that Howard nicely supports. Howard lays the days out in countable stacks. René will have supper each night on time. He will fall asleep over his newspaper. The next day he will return to the hospital to more livers. The livers will never change. The severed body parts are constant; only the names of their owners alter. Howard becomes privy to new and more malignancies. A breast here, a prostate there. Neatly labeled petri dishes: the tissues are, like the days, in countable stacks. Maybe a staff meeting intervenes. Perhaps he and his colleagues quibble over research-lab space. Or first authorship on scientific papers. Or access to new, noninvasive monitoring equipment. And then René, again. And supper again. And then René in bed again. He tucks in his son. He pulls the sheets up to his little chin. He covers him with his special blankie, and kisses him squarely on the forehead. Even as a small boy, everyone says that his son is a devilishly handsome little lady-killer.

"A baby," he says under his breath. Of course he wants a baby. Maybe three or four babies. Of course he wants a family. But now? He is still a baby himself. He doesn't really want to do anything—this is the secret no one knows. What will Howard do with a whimpering infant and a precocious eighteen-year-old wife, an unfulfilled graduate student, a wannabee chemist or maybe a zoologist? His outstanding selfishness. To marry René without being able to support her is ludicrous. Even if she follows her geology or biochemistry inclinations, she won't bring in any money for five years. With a baby she won't make a cent for six or seven years. And should she really have to study analytical chemistry to ward off starvation—or because pursuit of zoology is too much of a luxury? Howard's not ready for love and marriage—he may never be. The muse is sourness in his mouth and saliva suddenly evokes in him a strange dislike for his life. The little boy with black curly hair and charming smile will scream. Howard will finish medical school—or maybe he won't. And then he will be an intern—or maybe he won't. And then he'll pick a residency at a fine hospital—or maybe he won't. And then he'll specialize in kidneys or livers, breasts or the anus—or maybe he won't. Kidneys? They make him think of Leon Bloom. Livers or brains? Skin and bones, carpals and tarsals, metacarpals and metatarsals. Choking, he feels constrained, without a choice. But without any choice how can he possibly be a man?

Would the most generous act be his? Would it be one of supreme selfishness? Is it selfless or selfish to help her rid them both of the problem? Andy Carelli's old girlfriend had no trouble in Puerto Rico. The doctor had told Carelli to get lost but to come back in an hour. When he returned—after the hour in a nearby bar outperspiring his bottle of beer—the girl was gone. Carelli figured that he'd have to pray again since probably she was already dead. An hour later, half a mile away, Carelli said, he had found her alone, blithely sunning herself on the beach. No, the Puerto Rico solution is too facile: too expensive, too time-consuming. Too much effort, too late.

Howard looks absently at the stack of books above his desk. His attention strays to one particular title. Howard will take care of everything.

Before he sees René tonight, Howard makes a list of what he needs: a speculum, a vacurette, and a simple aspirator. He remembers where they are kept and decides to borrow the aspirator, vacuum pump, and sterilizer from the physiology lab. The sterilizer, really an autoclave, is too cumbersome, too large. He'll look strange to anyone who sees him leave the building with it. He decides to use his pressure cooker instead. He will bring up the pressure twice on the tongs, speculum, and vacurette to kill the spore-formers. Double boiling? What's it called again? The fact that the second boil kills

Bacillus and *Clostridium* as well as any nonspore-former contaminant? The vacuum pump needs a three-way adapter, which he will easily buy on Fifty-third Street. He'll need the reference book in the Billings library; he recalls flipping through it once. The four or five pages in question were the most well-worn. He opens the gyno-obstetrics textbook again.

"I strive to be mentally purged of prejudice." It is nighttime as they sit together on his stained sofa. They still hold hands. "Buddhism helps me do that. A great Buddhist sage and a youth sought the truth, they say. Some young guy traveled all over the world in search of their truth. They looked for the greatest of teachers. The young guy came into the room of his Zen master and explained his search. The sage bade him sit and asked him if he'd like some tea. The teacher started pouring. He filled up the young man's cup but he kept going. The sage just kept pouring while tea, of course, flowed all over the floor. The student cried out and told the wise man to stop. The sage continued to pour until the pot emptied. The floor was soaking wet. The Buddhist sat down before his own empty cup. He looked serenely at the surprised student. He waited. The young man asked, 'Why didn't you stop pouring?' The sage answered, 'We must rid ourselves of our preconceived concepts.'" Howard pauses. "René," he sighs after a moment, "Zen is the answer to my preconceived notions."

Each time her initial nervous excitement is dashed by Howard's crazy arbitrariness. She pleads with him to be consistent—a consistent lover, a consistent roommate, a consistent teacher—or at least consistently on time. He's not. "If you insist on consistency, you will block all communication between us," he quips. And means it. Since little conversation remains, and little of the first infatuation, René increasingly feels hopeless and desperate in his presence. Yet despite herself, she finds his nutsy preoccupation with cultural relativism as charming as his little-boy curly-black-hair earnest look. She can't help herself. She still counts the hours and minutes that are left before they will have an opportunity to make love. Some women can transcend their biology; she can. Howard removes her obstacles. She savors complicity, her bonds to him.

"Isn't it dangerous?" she asks. "Do you really know what you're doing?"

"Really, it's very easy—no risk at all in spite of what the zealots want us to believe. The medical rumors they spread around just bolster their outmoded theological beliefs. It's simple. Even painless. It will take me ten minutes." His authority precludes pleading. He tickles her side as antidote but his underlying certainty is not compromised. She knows he is seldom certain about anything—she respects for once the fact of the firmness of his decision. "You've helped me realize something I've been struggling with for a long time, René." His voice is a hush. "I've decided to become an obstetrician. I don't want to work with sick people at all. Ever, if I can help it."

Later, before dawn, he will walk jauntily on Sixty-third Street. Even the El will be silent. Unlike Florence or Atlantic City, no street cleaners push brooms while they gossip. No one will be there to clean streets. The streets will stay dirty. The bars, closed for their brief rest, will not yet have opened their doors to the hardened, the incorrigible, and the clandestine.

Howard will pass a coffee shop overlit with blank fluorescent lighting. And the veteran waitress will easily distinguish her drowsy customers from either side of the day. She will pour coffee punitively. The silty clay-gray water will run off each cup into its saucer. A clepsydra will mark sunless hours. A stumbling bum will pass by, unlit cigarette dangling. Everything within Howard's sight will be lymph gray, pus gray, even his coat. A crazed display window will vie with Eichhorn's Furs, a For Rent sign, and with anonymous steel-shuttered doorways, shops and signs—For Sale, Levitt's Jewelry. Howard thinks of the storefront Jesus revival halls providing sanctuaries in back for large families with pathetic snot-nosed children. Howard is reminded of cockroaches (*Blatta*), or bees (*Apies*), or mound-making termites (*Macrotermes*). He senses the hum of teeming life, the insect urban ecosystem, the attine ants with their instinctive plodding routine and without aspiration, bound to each other by necessity and chemical cues.

A stilted drawing in purple crayon, dirty and torn, flutters in the breeze. It rests in his path, then skitters away before he can read its detail. A political handbill eyeless with half a smiling head tumbles after it. Howard passes two large waste containers, sentinels on their adjacent corners. Both are red, white, and blue. Each bears large, block letters. They say exactly the same thing: HELP KEEP YOUR CITY CLEAN. He obliges. He throws the package, beginning to leak, into the leftmost can.

GASES
(Raoul)

In the same way with all other things:
Rivers and leaves and forage are
Transformed to animals, and animals to men,
And our own bodies oftentimes sustain
The strength of predatory beasts and birds.
Nature turns all the foods to living flesh
And out of this creates all sentient things.

Lucretius 98–55 BC (?) *De rerum natura*,
p. 31 in *The Nature of Life, Readings in Biology*,
The Great Books Foundation, Chicago, IL, 2001

In May 1937 Raoul Gautier celebrates his eighth birthday. Berthe Gautier, his grandmother, is grumbling as usual. The day-trip by train, small hand in gnarled hand, taking them to their destination: a point over which the largest object ever to fly would pass. The new zeppelin, the *Hindenburg,* is Raoul's obsession. Since his seventh birthday he has drawn zeppelins, flown paper zeppelins, and noticed all words that began with "Z." The *Graf Zeppelin*, its smaller sister ship, flies elite passengers; German noblemen, Swiss diplomats, and American tycoons criss-cross the sky to America and back. The first transatlantic air service thrills the boy. He wants to fly. Surely Grandmama will buy his *Hindenburg*'s transatlantic voyage ticket. Just that morning he saw her unfold bills and stack coins stashed in the cookie jar.

His imaginary journey takes three weeks. The airship zooms over 100 kilometers per hour to land in New York in three days. On the prevailing winds, the *Hindenburg* wafts back in two. Raoul closes his eyes: he always flies the silvery spare airship from France to America in silent motion. Other passengers, if any, are out of in sight. Raoul lies face down on the zeppelin's belly. Nothing below blocks his view. If, to Raoul the seascape at night means absolute peace, to his one wrinkled-face snore-vibrating bunkmate it is this same black sea surface that spells horror. The seamless tar of the open ocean drives the old man, sleepless, into the confusion of the smoking room. All bulk is above Raoul—but it is *negative* weight. It pulls him up, makes him weightless. "Takeoff, vertical and silent—unpowered by any engines," the old man whispers. "Let me simply see the world slowly fall away." And later: "Everything was motionless, except the wisps of clouds."

The new zeppelin, named for General von Hindenburg, conjurs the titanic stoical face of the old Prussian warlord who, himself, was the president of all Germans after World War I. Hindenburg, military uniform and polished medals, towered more than a foot over his diminutive successor, Adolph Hitler. Hindenburg, mustachioed round head in a spiked helmet, body stuffed into his armored greatcoat like a bratwurst into its casing, was a fitting namesake for the puffed-up airship. Politics, however, mean nothing to Raoul. His wonder, untouched by the giant swastikas on the zeppelin's tail, is at the largest object to fly before and maybe even since.

Berthe, grandmother, frets beneath her breath. Why does her good French boy want to see this "Nazi wonder"? Too kindhearted to deny him the glory of the zeppelin but not too much to grouse about it, she dares not mention her incessant preoccupation with the swastika. The Jewishness shadowed Raoul in the belly of the *Hindenburg.*

What are Jews, Raoul has wondered, watching his mother, the sturdy working-class plodder from the Midi, who neither practiced nor even mentioned Judaism. Each Sunday, like most everyone else in Sézanne, she dragged herself to mass inside the 400-year-old cathedral. If she did not look like a Champaignoise, at least no one assumed she was anything but an ordinary southerner. She did not interfere with the assumptions of the provincial Sézannaises. This strategy fit with her husband's Belgian Walloons, eager to be as French as possible. The *Kristallnacht* three years before had shattered more than glass; it had cut open the family's fabric, letting out a fearsome secret to enervate and vascularize, a social cancer.

Raoul memorized all he heard about the obese dirigible. Newspapers, magazines, and even an illustrated booklet for small boys depicted Hindenburg the man and the *Hindenburg,* the zeppelin. Berthe dismissed as propaganda the zeppelin comic book. The *Hindenburg* dirigible, 245 meters in length and forty-one meters in diameter, fit only with difficulty inside a football stadium. Above the Atlantic it cruised with hilltops and mountain peaks, silent at an altitude of between 200 and 300 meters. It rose as high as 1,400 meters above the sea to flee inclement weather or seek favorable winds.

In his mind, Raoul rides the belly of the *Hindenburg* itself and once he even built his own zeppelin 2. Helium, a cubic meter's worth, holds a kilogram aloft. A one-boy twenty-four-kilo zeppelin would have to extend ten meters in length by two meters in diameter. His calculations reckoned the weight of the rigid shell and counted three kilos for a boy-sized aluminum stretcher to bolt along the belly bottom. It must be large enough and comfortable enough to permit Raoul to gaze out on his front or back at the Earth beneath. The sprocket, pedals, and chain from his bicycle, attached to the rotor of his mother's electric fan, he figured, would provide propulsion. He planned daily flights. His zeppelin precluded boredom and bullies. When threatened he ran out to the bloated monster and simply flew away. The dirigible, stationed at the edge of the grass in the play park, always idle, always lay in wait for him.

Berthe and Raoul transfer at Paris. They alight, wait and reboard. The clanky train clacks toward the northern crest of France where zeppelins glide en route from the Frankfurt aerodrome and the American airship base at Lakehurst, New Jersey. Like clockwork, the zeppelins rose and Nazis landed at their anticipated arrival time. Foul weather and unpredictable winds merely hardened their resolve. Raoul and his grandmother stepped off the platform one hour before the scheduled zeppelin pass. They coursed the market, stocked up on olives and a baguette. In the moist fog, hand in hand, they found their way down to the shore and awaited the arrival of the largest airship in Christendom.

Anxiety and expectation. Dread, thrill, and impatience. Boredom. Half an hour later Raoul scans the horizon nearby. Does wind and weather so alter the zeppelin course as to render it invisible from the beach? He looks down the beach, stalks the coastline with his sharp vision.

He is startled by a dark mass that suddenly looms over the

dune to the right. It moves fast. Dreamlike, there is no question, none at all, that it is real. A cellar closes over him. The dull metallic-gray *Hindenburg* emerges as he goggles, and it slides rapidly over his head. Guy wires hull-dangling surprise Raoul. The sleek hull streams toward him over his head, no, on his head as if daring him to leap aboard. The bone-deep hum of the diesels surprise him too. He had expected an effortless sail, silent and beyond human concern. The aluminum cabin molded along its belly is articulated with countless slanting windows. They look out and down, to give the impression of scale. Raoul's head swims. The zeppelin already passes over him. The frantic pang that it is so soon gone gives way to his mood descent, here now, forever completed, the greatest moment so far of his young life. He turns as the giant gray shape heads out over the channel, the bullet nose and pilot's windows lost forever to cloud and wind. The clean, futuristic craft and its foreshortened swastikas dominate the tailplanes in black and wine-red.

The anticlimactic stop in Paris on the return is dull and routine—until grandmother Berthe buys him the blue balloon. As they walk in step, Raoul spots bouncing colors. From the place de la Concorde they now approach the garden. He leads her by his warm hand through the jardin des Tuileries. They promenade along the gravel paths among the people, toy boats, organ grinders, and peanut vendors, as Gauls do every Sunday. She says nothing to the small boy— juden, juif, juive, Judenkind, isroyal, Israel, shalom, montjuich, Yiddish, juden Swine—whose hand she holds. Grandmama and boy in their small way resist the war. Red, rose, blue, yellow, and green bubbles bounce higher than birds. Buffeted by wind, they frolic silently. The sky is dimming at dusk.

The boy slips from his grandmother's grip so quickly that her voice does not follow. Later she scolds him. For years she scolds whoever listens. The balloon story, not the *Hindenburg* sighting, firmly ensconced in the family archive, joins one hundred retold stories sharper than memories. Raoul runs toward the bobbing colored balloons. The big red-nosed vendor does not smile as he opens the valve from time to time, filling a balloon. The desperate, imaginative child watches in awe as each balloon tugs and strains to escape from the swivel tap.

Gone are the pigeons, people, and perambulators. The valve opens. Then shuts. Opens, then shuts. Each balloon snaps toward the sky, cloudy moonlit even though now darkness prevails. Raoul is leaning on the tank, his cheek against the cold cylinder. Grandmama sighs, pants, beats her breast as—at last—she catches sight of him. She verifies for herself that he is not dead. "Thanks be to God," she mutters. To him, to the balloon man and to every inattentive person, she cries, "Looking everywhere for him, very bad boy, for an hour." Her slapping hands are angrier than the folds around her mouth. She chides him in a running volley; tweaks his ear. But she cannot refuse to buy the big blue balloon. The balloon represents their unspoken Sunday pact; it commemorates their tiny resistance.

Raoul supervises its inflation. He had selected carefully the one he wanted filled for its darker, thicker looking blueness. The vendor puffs it deftly onto the nozzle. Raoul holds his breath. The vendor turns the valve, initiates the wheeze of a balloon coming to life. As it wiggles and puffs, it grows lighter blue, sky blue. Raoul's pride swells with the balloon; he wants it to keep inflating to be larger than the others, but he doesn't want it to slip and fly off. Finally the vendor shushes the valve and slides the balloon, translucent and perfect, free of the tank. The rubber complains as the vendor's thick fingers twist the end around the way his grandmother twists the necks of fat pullets. Frowning, the man lets the balloon loose and it struggles up toward the sky, wiggling its tail, until the string brings it up short. He bends to hand it to Raoul. "It's past time for me to go home," he complains, "and you too."

The balloon survives the night train ride home. Raoul runs straightaway into his cubbyhole of a room. He lets go the string even before Grandmama removes her shoes and rubs her swollen feet. He holds his breath, hopping on one foot, pleading with the balloon to rise. The balloon floats to the ceiling of his tiny closet-room. Raoul intently watches. He silently wills it upwards and begs it to live there successfully for many days.

Morning light shines on the blue balloon first. Pulling on the string, Raoul brings it to himself. Reluctantly buoyant, each day the blue balloon withers more. One day it descends. Yet it remains inflated in the corner. Finally it collapses and dies, a crumple of rubber on the soiled floor.

The war years are lonely for the boy. Janine, his older sister, who lives in Brussels with an aunt and uncle, fades from his memory. His mother, haggard and harassed, shares with him no news from his father. Grandmama, lively and strong, remains housebound. His back against his closet-room wall,

Raoul outlines insects, birds, and bats. He makes paper air-planes. Safely inside himself, he occasionally shows his flying creatures to his grandmother. His tiny family, unrooted in Sézanne, lacks the natural connections of the Sézannais. Unrelated by blood, marriage, or work, these Gautiers are not now and never will be *Sézannais communité*.

Sézanne changed little in five centuries. Beneath ponderous stone buildings lie a network of tunnels that connect the *caves*. Families store their wine and perishables in their *caves*. From any sizable house one can descend into a low, rough-hewn burrow fitted with niter and caches of wine. Champagne and brandy rest in racks in alcoves among several branchings, some sloping or dropping down still farther toward sous-cellars of other houses. If one knows the labyrinth, one can meander across the entire town with no emergence above ground. Many boys first smoke, first make love, first drink unto stupor in their fathers' *caves*. Raoul is terrified of the damp subcity. He hates his *devoir*, his duty to fetch the *vin ordinaire* for each meal. He slowly creeps alone into the moist darkness of the first chamber. On the descent he snatches the first unlabeled bottle within reach, stacked next to the onions. He runs upstairs seeking light and air. He has panicked and tripped. He has broken bottles on the stones. He has suffered scorn and scoldings.

Medieval legends abound. Neighbor Claude's *cave* connects to an unused wing of Raoul's father's. Raoul is accused by Claude of sneaky theft of a good bottle of Bordeaux. Claude says the tunnel construction has to do with taxes. Once the Germans come, though, they will be used to hide Jews bundled together, mostly in the dark.

Their pale faces will peer and squint like moles at Berthe's lamp when she brings the nearest family a daily meal or a candle. For Raoul, theirs will be a hidden layer of the life of Sézanne. The nightmare, forgotten each morning, revives with renewed vigor each night. Raoul fears the *cave* more than he fears any German. The German threat is the threat of interment in the *cave*. His mother's secret Jewishness becomes his ticket to an unspeakable future, the haggard and silent life of the *cave*.

Perfunctorily when alone, and ostentatiously under his grandmother's watchful eye, Raoul completes his school-work. The dates of the second and third Republic, the conjugation of irregular verbs, the remote *passé* unused. Balzac, Daudet, Bourget, and physical exercise. The sound of the German tongue fills him with dread, *Hindenburg* pride, and longing for his father. Raoul's days are endless exercises in perseverance. The languages he memorizes worry him. Latin reinforces his loneliness, English is unpronounceable, and German pains his soul.

Football after class is less tolerable still: forced camaraderie, a hustling body strain, and the cold sweat of fear. Football is the domain of Gaspar, Raymond, Jean-Paul, and Thomas, adolescent fascists all. They despise Jews and Communists, anticipate the burning of books, brag about their achievements: thievery and wicked kicks to small boys. They heckle girls. They yell in unison as they scramble boisterously towards Raoul. A roiling corps of limbs, mouths, and ruddy flesh, they taunt, "We're going to get you! Ha, ha, ha!" What they like best, in short (he knows from his father and grandmother) is just what Nazis do. Raoul evades all butcher boys by immersion in billows, clouds, and gas. On the football pitch he runs continually but always parallel to the action. Never converging on it, he eyes the white and protean clouds that drift abroad in the Champagne sky—until Gaspar's kick to his kneecap. The ground slaps him. He lies tasting soil, smelling blood. Sweat chills his damp jersey as he rolls to watch clouds while he catches his breath. The *moniteur* shouts into his revery. He wipes his face with a sleeve, rolls up to trot, and rejoins the surging play.

Indoors, the secondary school student Raoul learns that everything, including life, is made of molecules. He fills his copybooks with the physics teacher's notes on atoms, molecules, protons, electrons, and the chemical bond. Monsieur Perrier, topped with graying, bushy hair, wears a ruffled shirt. Raoul scans M. Perrier's veiny hands and sad, sweet smile. He asks the teacher: "How do scientists know about molecules? How can you show that atoms exist?"

The sunlight pierces the particles of dust in the classroom afternoon air. M. Perrier answers his question. "Gases give the best clues to atoms. The existence of atoms," he adds, "can be deduced from gases. The same amount of gas of different kinds weighs differently, each according to its kind. Hydrogen is the lightest gas and helium weighs a bit more. Oxygen and nitrogen are heavier still. Do you understand?"

Raoul already knows about gases. Nitrogen fills the large tank in the chemistry laboratory. Oxygen, burned out under a bell jar in such a way as to cause a mouse to suffocate for lack of it, is required for breathing. Carbon dioxide is sighed out by both Mama and Grandmama Berthe. Hydrogen and helium: hydrogen weighs less, but is explosive while helium is noble; it doesn't interact.The Germans had dared use hydrogen when the Americans refused to sell them helium. Just days after Raoul's zeppelin spotting, the *Hindenburg* victims paid dearly for this, their daring error, their blustery arrogance. Hydrogen, hydrogen, the fuel of the universe; it was hydrogen that exploded the zeppelin. Nobel helium by contrast had raised Raoul's blue balloon until it finally succumbed to air. What can gas weigh?

A hundred times Raoul peruses the periodic table in the textbook. Hydrogen is one and helium is two. Nitrogen is seven and oxygen is eight. In oxygen, as a gas, two atoms are present in one molecule, not just one. But what are these numbers? Just numbers?

Raoul ponders. The great boulders, the oaks and poplars, the budding breast of Marie-Jeanne and flat front of Françoise. How can all these be made of atoms? Chemistry books and physics teachers provoke him. Science is real-world experiment, description, ideas. No, Raoul thinks, these different substances, the cleat on Gaspar's shoe and Marie-Jeanne's nipple, could never be gas. This can't be the same stuff. Something is hidden in these numbers, something exciting and beautiful, something he longs to understand.

To clear his head, Raoul spends much time at an airy retreat. He scampers to the summit of a large, flat-topped boulder, too steep to climb on one side, accessible only from the rear. Glaciers of 18,000 years ago, retreating, pushed the huge erratic no farther. One monadnock stolidly emerges several hundred meters behind his house. As sun rays stab into the darkness of the forest on long afternoons, Raoul's interest focuses beyond the dust particles, on the invisible flow of gases. He contemplates size from his secret rocky seat. He attempts to count the particles of dust. But gases are not dust. They are made of atoms. And atoms are particles unimaginably tinier than dust. How can anyone see the atoms of a gas?

How many atoms to see? The textbook declares that Avogadro's number, 6.022×10^{23} is a count of atoms; this huge unmanageable number must be memorized. Why? Because it is the number of atoms in a mole, any mole. And a mole? A mole is the standard number of atoms that occupy the same volume of each gas. A mole of gas weighs in grams the same as the atom's atomic weight. A mole of gas, therefore, is a special amount. Twelve grams for carbon. Only one for hydrogen. Four grams for helium, as much as a coin. Yet it floats into the air as it if had *negative* weight. A mole of gas under normal conditions in France occupies 22.4 liters of space. Take a sack. Fill it with gas without forcing it, like holding a bag above a balloon vendor's stopcock. The helium flows upwards to fill it. Be sure the sack holds just the special volume, 22.4 liters at standard temperature and pressure. The bag would contain some 602,200,000,000,000,000,000,000 molecules.

Weigh the gas. A mole of pure hydrogen (H) will weigh one gram. Molecular hydrogen (H_2) will weigh two grams. Molecular nitrogen (N_2) will weigh fourteen grams. Molecular oxygen (O_2) will weigh sixteen grams.

Raoul's last memory of Sézanne will have been of gases and weights, the serendipitous accident of verifying the laws of nature to himself. And his focused eureka never faded.

Buying large, colored balloons, he practices filling them without stretching. Since a mole's worth, 22.4 liters, was too large, he divides everything by ten. Next he collects gases. At the clinic the physician draws liquid nitrogen from his large tank to burn off warts. Frozen nitrogen, the man had explained, really works to remove warts, even from children, nearly painlessly. Doctor Roquet, a *soi-disant* scientist, enthusiastically supplies Raoul with oxygen and nitrogen. Roquet tells him to read Pascal; a little treatise, *On the Weight of the Air*. He explains that Pascal explains how gas has weight. Indeed, gases have weight even if they rise. Engravings show experiments that any seventeenth-century amateur philosopher can easily perform on decorated pages. Roquet lends him three stout cylinders and bids him return with the outcome of his "excellent experiments." Raoul collects the liquid nitrogen, which bubbles furiously enough, in fact, to pop the cork stopper.

The hydrogen and the second stock of nitrogen come from the tanks in M. Perrier's chemistry lab. Silent M. Perrier smiles at Raoul's enthusiasm. For the third nitrogen, Raoul burns the oxygen out of an air sample with a candle. He collects the remaining gas through water with a rubber tube. Oxygenless air, explains the textbook, is more than 99 percent nitrogen. Helium takes him a month to obtain, all supplies from the United States have ceased. He finally coaxes grandmama to buy it from a tawdry balloon vendor on a cool Sunday at the market's edge in Rheims.

Raoul hides his equipment and calculations. He stashes everything in the garden shed. His mother is, as usual, unobservant. His grandmother's eyes are watchful. To weigh the gases Raoul fashions a small metal hook with many prongs, upon which he hangs the gas sacks. He rummages through the storage bins in the wine cellar. He finds a pair of fine antique scales. Methodically, he lists in order all the wine-cellar weights—all too heavy for the gases.

Raoul remembers the Ashanti gold weights. Not made of gold but bronze to weigh against gold. In the English class-room cabinet, Mr. Stanley stores two rows of varied Ashanti gold weights that gather dust. Some tiny, some very large and decorative, all weights. Three are double crocodiles with shared stomachs, two flat-headed twins, seven long-tailed lizards and one a Kumasi chieftain's stool. Made in the nine-teenth century. All are from the Gold Coast Colony of the British Crown. Ashanti weights are precise grams, multiples or easy fractions of grams.

Raoul requests and happily is granted the weights on loan from Mr. Stanley. In the shortening dusk of late afternoons, Raoul weighs standards. He uses the best analytical balance in Sézanne; the one in M. Perrier's chemistry lab. He cali-brates Ashanti gold weights against the known bronze weights lined up in the cherry box. Raoul marks labels on white adhesive tape with fine black ink. He stows the cali-brated weights in a wine crate in the garden shed. For each lizard-, cross-, or cube-decorated Ashanti weight, Raoul records its value in grams next to its name: "serpent," "twin" and "skinny-lizard," and their sixteen brethren. He lists the weight descriptions in order, from light to heavy, in his blue notebook. His grandmother demands to know what is in his notebook. He shrugs, claims he is doing nothing. She agrees. "If you're not doing anything with your hands, you're doing nothing." His mother, so fatigued and distracted, never notices what he does.

Raoul reads Pascal's little treatise in a single sitting. The library has a facsimile edition, complete with strange seventeenth-century spelling, letters *s* that looked like *f*. Pascal's own woodcuts decorate the pages, some uncut. Curved glass tubes like alp-horns full of quicksilver, siphons and pumps manned by disembodied hands wearing ruffled lace cuffs. By experiment, Pascal proved that the air has a measurable weight that presses equally on things at the same altitude. He compared air to water that presses on the fish of the sea. He wrote that he could, by pressure measurements at progressive altitudes, "find the exact extent of the air's sphere and of the vapors called the atmosphere." The total height of the atmosphere presses on the sea with as much weight as does a column of water thirty-one feet and two inches in height. The creation of a vacuum by opening a fireplace bellows with the holes sealed could lift a column of water thirty-one feet high and as wide as the bellows. The air presses us with this much weight, presses Raoul's balloons of lighter gas to rise like air bubbles in a pond.

A cheerful, bright spring day comes mercifully restful and without wind. Yet Raoul sees the air. In the shed, he fills his balloons in sequence with different kinds of gas, some barely to ambient pressure. Four thicker skinned beige ones he pumps to capacity to use as stores to fill the others—red hydrogen, blue helium, green nitrogen.

First he tries a Pascal experiment. He takes in turn red, blue, and green spherical balloon to measure its circumference. Each averages 465 millimeters. Then he walks with them, the happy child out alone for a stroll, to the only rise in walking distance; across the river. He climbs to the crest, a scant 200 meters above the valley. He measures again. They average 468. He detects the difference, the expanding from air pressure. Exhilarated, he is transformed. He has become Pascal himself, reborn.

The next day, a Saturday, rucksack filled, he returns, sneakily, to his airy retreat. He climbs the flat-topped boulder, scales in one hand, gas balloons in the other. His pockets jangle with bronze Ashanti weights. He notes the fluid pale blue air and reads its balminess—23.6 centigrade—on the thermometer he has mounted on the tree trunk. Atop his ancient hill, where a silhouette in the wind is boulder that serves as launch pad for his balloons, Raoul leaves war and insane warriors below.

He hooks each balloon on its strong thread loop to nicely aligned nails that protrude from the tree. Each bobs, near eye level, on the black oak.

The hanging, flaccid balloons are weighed directly. The levity of each fat source balloon should be the difference between the weight of an equivalent balloon filled with air and the volume of the source balloon times the density of the gas. He weighs each flaccid balloon on the scale. Ah, repeatability. Each is the weight of last time, and the time before. Each measures out correctly. Then he hangs weights from the strings of each source balloon in turn until each hangs suspended, floating in equilibrium, before his face. He weighs the green globe twice. He uses a weight of different shape each time. He grabs the blue globe that bobs upward. Glancing at his entries, Raoul now delirious with success. He takes the blue balloon and, in memory of his earlier companion, this balloon's ancestor, he lets it go, conscious of the relief of liberation.

Silent and smooth as a zeppelin, the blue globe rises. He watches it move through denser gases, stays with it until it leaves him behind and disappears. He imagines the balloon's eye view lost in the bottomless sky. The Earth recedes through its blue depth. The balloon expands as it rises to rarer heights. This bubble of helium expands triumphantly until, soaring unseen, it bursts its latex chamber. Free but no longer an individual, the balloon's innards rejoin the gases of the atmosphere.

Shouts penetrate Raoul's reverie. He sees Gaspar and his cohort. They see him. Amid his equipment, notebooks, balloons, hooks, balance, all gathered with such care, he sinks embarrassed. Moreover, he is ashamed to feel embarrassed about what so recently had been such a source of pride. Snickering at a distance, they stop. They listen. They leer. Raoul is exposed, no use caching Ashanti gold weights, bags, notes, and balances. His heart pounds, blood rises to his pulsing head. He rips the two crosshatched pages of data from his notebook, folds them into a triangular lump, and wedges it into his trousers coin pocket. Snatching the weights from the balance and the ground he stuffs them into his socks.

The noisy warriors are almost upon him. They scramble upwards, yelling. Gaspar carries a knotty stick. The three behind bear clubs and small branches. Raoul sees the jeering faces. Thomas, Raymond, Jean-Pierre follow their intrepid leader, singing. Their words become distinct, audible, later to embed in memory like a sliver of word, infected. "Loud ring out the cheers, flags all waving, truth and justice wins over all, over all, over all."

"Look," taunts Thomas. "He's playing with balloons!"

"Maybe he's sending signals to the enemy," says Jean-Pierre.

"If we let him go, maybe he too will fly," cries Gaspar. "Forward—march!"

Raoul kicks up bits of dried grass and stones. He tries first to save the bronze scales by burial. Can he risk it? Dare he jump from the boulder's steep side? He pleads to the sun to transport him to the outer realms. He begs its brilliance and omnipotent energy to shrink him to microscopic dimensions. While the four rowdies defile his boulder lab, he enjoins the sun to convert him to an atom—not dust, just a single tiny atom.

"Get him," Gaspar screams. "He's a traitor, a traitor. As bad as any dirty Jew. Do you try to fly, wou-wou? Let's help him fly!"

Raoul is penetrated by their noise. He remembers nothing but it receding. He is rocked back and forth. "*Un, deux, trois!*" High, low. Heave ho. He is released, and floats up, dizzy, then down, arms and legs flailing, breath lost. Then a splash of pain across the face. Darkness. The fall, it was said, ceased abruptly on the jagged rock. His face was his landing gear. His body impacts the welcoming soft soil. Dry leaves scattered.

The scar takes years to heal, but it never heals, never really heals. The gap is sewn, but Doctor Roquet arrives too late to stitch it properly. The wound is so ugly that his snickering schoolmates and teachers turn away from him. His face is an open gash for weeks and a throbbing sore for months. His dark eyes and brown hair offer compensation for the raw disfigurement of his left cheek. Françoise reassures him that he will regain his looks. A puckered seam that mocks indelibly the right side of his handsome face remains.

The notebook pages are saved. Not a single gold weight is lost; the balance only jostled.

The summer he turns seventeen, 1946, Raoul constructs a gas chromatograph, a box full of coiled tubes to measure smelly hydrogen sulfide. At the final school assembly M. Perrier awards him the prize, a scholarship to study chemistry at the university of the center of the world: Paris V. As he ascends the auditorium stage, embarrassed, Raoul stumbles. His performance in English, electricity and magnetism, in computing and organic chemistry is adequate. In the chemistry of gases he excels.

Disdainful and silent at social gatherings, Raoul becomes more voluble when surrounded by scientific colleagues. Even the women claim he is prisoner in a house of gases. His acquaintances nickname him "the monk." At age twenty-four, Raoul is hired by the Institute for Atmospheric Research, in Chicago. Scarcely aware that this United States institute is funded by the military, he thrives. His technical skills are valued by atmospheric chemists, his help sought by colleagues. He designs chromatographs, exquisitely sensitive devices to separate gases, and mounts them in stratospheric airplanes. His instruments line the decks of ocean-going ships. He rapidly becomes known as the most competent and valuable young chemist at the institute.

Pollution research and environmental science are the popular tunes of the early seventies, and they are well funded. But Raoul, naïve and ambitious, considers the environmental trends "soft." He claims "environmental science" has been invented to assuage, that it is reactionary. If environmental science is a misnomer, "environmental studies" is an even worse sham. Scientists, Raoul asserts, must pose a clear question answerable by experiment. If the atmosphere is ill and if it functions by an unknown physiology, how can environmental impact studies or money cure it?

Raoul avoids teamwork; he works alone or, at most, with a student or two, or a colleague. He seeks research opportunities. His Paris V doctoral thesis, "Measurement of dimethyl sulfide and dimethyl sulfoxide over the Atlantic Ocean," published late, brings him international attention. He is never comfortable in Chicago—it is always too hot, too cold, too wet, too dry, too loud, too windy, or too something else. So, when offered membership in the research team at the Institute for Atmospheric Chemistry, not quite in Paris but on the suburban train line at Gif-sur-Yvette, he proudly accepts.

Site of the intellectual and scientific community around Paris, the reputation of Gif for serious research far transcends that of the university system. The senior scientist, Guy Leysson, protects Raoul from his first day at the lab bench. Leysson assigns him few formal duties, and appoints him chief of the research equipment and its team, a way to encourage Raoul's exquisite touch. Routinely Gautier deploys the equipment on the Mediterranean cruises. Grateful for his freedom at the bench and in the open air,

Raoul's devotion to duty is so intense that Leysson never has to defend his decision to leave him alone.

Raoul's life is good but unremarkable until the freon explosion.

"Stratospheric sink for chlorofluromethanes" is published in 1974 in the widely read British scientific weekly, *Nature*. Freon, mostly dichlorofluoromethane, released from everyone's refrigerator and freezer all around the globe, spills into the atmosphere, destroying ozone. The alarm set off by this dry work—two boring pages written by two Californians, Dolina and Mowland—is unexpected. The arcane study of atmospheric gas catapults into media consciousness worldwide. The ethereal comes down to Earth, has an immediate practical impact on the global environment. Preoccupation with human health twists the innocent heart of scientific inquiry toward new fears.

Money there is now, suddenly, for meetings. Every two years at the Naragansett campus, University of Rhode Island Marine Center, money will now flow to a world of atmospheric science, to experts in air chemistry. Why, just a few years earlier no one could afford any meetings, especially with French people. Especially was there no money for atmospheric chemistry meetings, an orphaned academic field anyway, one lacking tradition, substance, a base. This science enjoyed no home department since geologists, biologists, and chemists had all deemed it "out of their speciality" and meteorologists had weather predictions to make. They would not be deflected for such theoretical, maybe useless, scientific exercises.

Raoul is surprised by the fact that his corner of the globe, his quiet subvisible science, converts to Big Science. A sluice gate opens when funds pour forth. The Manufacturing Chemist's Society (MCS) advertizes in all the correct journals and newsletters. They will employ twelve atmospheric scientists in six weeks. Did such people even exist who, on demand, can perform the calculations, make the atmospheric ultraviolet and infrared measurements? Who can run an accurate chromatograph, then analyze a month's worth of data — and also make sense? Student fellowships for atmospheric chemistry, geophysics, and meteorology proliferate. Opportunities open up for travel to worldwide gas-monitoring station networks. Money is thrown directly at the question: "Does freon cause UV depletion cause cancer?"

In Providence, Rhode Island, in 1976, Gautier strains to understand his colleagues: articulate fast-talker Alton Brainerd; voluble, redheaded Stephen Ramsey; and jolly banal Don Peterson. He has worked with these men for years. He doesn't mind working with them—indeed he likes them—it is only the beer and pizza after their work sessions that he hates.

On their home ground under the garish lights of the Leaning Tower of Pizza, McDonald's arch in sight, in this relaxed autumn moment at a chipped formica red-checkered table laden with cheap beer, if the talk were limited to ocean sampling, solar spectra, the electron capture device of the gas chromatograph, Raoul would join in. Raoul, who prides himself on the quality of his spoken English, is uneasy with his fellow scientists if he isn't talking. Small talk, argot, slang, gossip, he deplores—only science can be tolerated. He glances around. He fingers two plastic wastebaskets that hold little squeezy packages of ketchup, mustard, and mayonnaise, a few tired French fries. "French fries"—he considers the expression as complimentary as the term "capôte anglais" for condoms.

Raoul stops trying to follow the chatty conversation of his fellows. He watches the rushed passersby, all unresponsive and so busy. He wants to leave, deplores the force to be sociable. Craving privacy, Raoul feels tongue-tied and exposed. He can't just leave his colleagues—he needs the car they rented together in Don Peterson's name. Alton Brainerd's sentences run along like a light opera libretto. Better not to understand the words; wiser to attribute to singers poetry worthy of the music. Suddenly Red Ramsey's words register.

"The guys that come to the meetings were good guys, sure, as long as you were working with them, but what else can they talk about but retention times, sensitivities, and peak heights?" Ramsey's eyes sparkle as they wander. He ogles passing skirts.

"What about Darly-James?" asks Brainerd, mindlessly tapping his spoon. "Not all analytical chemists are dull. Darly-James may be a gas chromatographer, but he's not boring."

Brainerd continues to tap. Peterson knocks over his half-full wine glass and reaches to pick it up, too late. Pretending it is nothing, he attempts to hide the spill and clean his trousers. Ramsey and Brainerd scramble for napkins to wipe him off. Raoul reaches over and silently pours salt on Peterson's lap. The others freeze and stare.

"Absorbing the wine—a very chemical solution," Brainerd chuckles. They laugh.

Steve Ramsey slaps Raoul on the back. The waitress comes

over tentatively to see Raoul salting Peterson's lap. She glances at their beer pitchers. Then Peterson asks, "Uh, what are you doing?" Raoul sputters, red-faced. More laughter. The waitress leaves, nervous. They try to recall the conversation in progress before the interruption.

"Come on, Row-ool," drawls Peterson. "We're just gassing you."

Raoul had thought that he knew all the American puns for gas, but this offense alarms him. To *gas someone,* transitively, as humorous, in a century when millions had been gassed, screams outrageous.

GEOSECS (Geochemical Oceans Section Studies), allegedly international, is controlled by the National Science Foundation of the United States. GEOSECS is the offspring of the International Decade of Ocean Exploration (IDOE). The initials IDOE feel alien to Gautier. As a chemist he feels out of place among oceanographers. He is a laboratory chemist, whereas IDOE is Very Big Science that works by committee. GEOSECS is Big Science subsumed by IDOE. Raoul hates committees. He despises being crammed into subcommittees, sub-sub-committees—each subcommittee meeting in a stuffy room. This incessant ineffective social nonsense halves his lab freedom, emasculates his working time.What he values most, his lebensraum for dedication to work, is diminished, shortened, and halved again. Like Zeno's tortoise-and-hare chase, money equals time and time is needed to spend it, worse, lavish amounts of time are needed to find money. Science freezes in a bureaucratic paradox, science is sacrificed; real science becomes the murdered victim. He craves the return to work. He yearns to work alone. But to work alone he needs Big Money, thus Big Science. Big Science needs him too.

"The freon thing has begun to die down, hasn't it, Gautier?" Red Ramsey asks, jerking Raoul toward the present. "Dolina and Mowland, real hustlers, those guys," Ramsey goes on. "Their computer models are absurdly over simplified. The UV effect can't be due only to freon 11 and 12. God knows there's carbon tetrachloride—nitrous oxide—lots of other stuff that gets up there into the stratosphere to break down ozone. UV has lots of ways of getting in. How can you make fancy calculations about stratospheric gases and UV when you don't even know what goes on up there? We published more than seven papers on this. But we don't take our abstracts to reporters at the *New York Times* or the *Washington Post*. Not only was photochemistry involved, but also there are coupling mechanisms and dynamics. They oversimplified everything in that article. But they sure did hit a raw nerve!"

Gautier feels infinite exhaustion as the ozone-UV-cancer topic begins again. Here, once more, begins another potentially painful conversation.

"You really showed them," Alton Brainerd smiles. "Your superb paper in the IJAR—you know, the *International Journal for Atmospheric Research*. They missed the methyl chloride, they had forgotten both the reactions of nitrous oxide, but boy, they couldn't miss it when you reanalyzed their shoddy measurements. My God. As you elegantly demonstrated, they should have taken all their measurements in constant frequency, but no! They followed each other like sheep and measured everything using constant current. They merely *assumed* that these damned freons show a linear response to concentration. Ha!" Alton sighs as Raoul grins weakly.

"What bothers me most," Brainerd goes on, "was that scientific fortunes and reputations were made and lost, traded like commodities on the Chicago Board of Trade. The sense of mercantilism that pervades the entire freon-ozone-UV mess really disturbs me."

"No," says Peterson, "I think they must know a whole lot more than you give them credit for, at least about the cancer-UV connection. They already put the UV-cancer stuff on the agenda for an entire morning session next summer at Wiesbaden."

Brainerd daubs at some ketchup with a fry. He munches. "Sure, if your specialty were UV and skin cancer, you and your physician friends would be furious. You'd join the critics and rage at the media, which glosses over the important details, especially on the medical and epidemiological part of the story."

"Oh, Christ, clinicians?" says Ramsey. "Don't tell me we have to listen to a parade of skin doctors, plastic surgeons, and cosmetologists now. Let them stick to making money off their balms, unguents, and poultices. An 'epidermis epidemic' would be the best thing that ever happened to them."

"The agenda for what?" Gautier asks. "What meeting next summer?"

The three Americans look at each other.

"They're planning a small—well, large enough—international meeting," Peterson explains. "A 'congress' they call it, on the 'Gases of the Atmosphere' at Wiesbaden next year.

It's like a *festshrift* to celebrate the retirement or the birthday or something—birthday, I think— of Klaus Brunger. You know him, the lab chief at the Max Planck Institute. Everyone's invited. They'll publish it in the IJAR. How come you don't know? You were invited, weren't you?"

"Who was invited from France?" says Gautier, a hint of resignation.

The three Americans, like school kids trying to hide their chewing gum, look to each other again. "Gautier," says Ramsey, "if you're not invited I'm sure no one from France is coming."

"Everyone I know who has already accepted the invitation to speak is from the U.S. or Germany," adds Alton Brainerd.

"No, some were from Great Britain. Darly-James is coming from England, I heard," says Don Peterson.

"But," says Gautier with a wry smile, "this is exactly what Americans mean when they say an 'international' meeting. Of course, it's euphemistic for 'pan-Anglophone,' which includes Germans who speak perfect English—as most Germans do. Inglo-Jermanic **A**tmospheric **R**esearch journal, is what we call the IJAR. The Inglo-Jermanic Atmosphere Research crowd is inhospitable to frogs and other skin-respiring animals." The Americans seem shocked now. "No, it's all right; I've worked long enough with you Americans to have a thick skin—a *frog* skin."

"I'll get you an invitation," says Ramsey. "I'm sure I can, I'm a member of Zeiloff's agenda committee. It still will be a few months before we're ready to send out the final version of the program."

"Write us both an invitation," says Raoul. "My boss, Guy

Leysson, will send me to the Wiesbaden congress even though I am only maître-de-recherche and he is directeur. He cannot tolerate us not to be represented. Even if he is obliged to pay for my voyage. Monsieur Leysson's reputation will suffer. Leysson knows, he had a good physics formation—he would attend only for the Rhine wine-tasting party. But he doesn't know the new things. Leysson needs me to understand the new results of the actual physicists. I'll go. I will present our new data from the North Atlantic."

"Won't Leysson retire soon?"

"God, no; he has at least ten years before mandatory retirement, though scientifically these days he doesn't do so much. But then, not many of the functionaries in our Institute do very much. Furthermore, some people think he's not entirely well either."

"There's you and your student. You two work," Don Peterson says. "And what about Girard Beaumont? He usually shows up at meetings."

"Beaumont? If it weren't for the Girard Beaumonts of the world, French science wouldn't be invited anywhere. Beaumont may come—it won't matter. You must invite him and invite Jules Farley, too, in any case, but don't worry—I will come to Wiesbaden. At least I don't anymore have to sign a statement that I will say my lecture only in French to receive travel money. Until a few years ago we were obliged to, you know."

"Beaumont speaks good English, real smooth. Will he be next in line after Leysson retires? Who will be the new director?" asks Peterson.

"Remember Leysson has probably ten more years, so isn't

too well known who's going to be the next director. Probably Jules Farley, he's older than Beaumont. But I don't know. Don't worry, nothing happens there very soon anyway."

Stephen Ramsey laughs. His blue eyes focus hard on Raoul. "Raoul, he's teasing you! Jules Farley doesn't speak two words of English. You're next in line yourself. You know that!"

"No, Red, I'm not. I work too hard. That's not always wise. And I don't socialize."

Raoul, back now from Weisbaden, a week after Jules Farley tells him, in confidence, that Gif's research director, Guy Leysson (only 52 years old), has an enlarged prostate that only Leysson's wife has ever mentioned, squats in the corner of his lab. He faces a coverless panel with a plastic tube in his mouth and a screwdriver in hand. Mlle. Rigaud (the common secretary for Jules Farley, Girard Beaumont, and even Raoul Gautier), fluffy and bouncy but curious as usual, trots into the lab with her high heels clicking. Because he is crouching she doesn't think he's there. She screeches in shrill soprano, "Monsieur Gautier, telephone. Long distance. Germany." Her voice doppler-drops as she rushes down the corridor toward the next open door, the next-door laboratory, a carpentry work shop.

"I'm here," he says, removing saliva-wet and toothmarked tubing from his mouth. "Who is it? I'm busy." Not gruff, just the usual firm. Incontrovertibly firm.

"It's a woman with an accent, English or American, I think. The call is from Tubingen or Munich."

"I'll take it," he says to Mlle. Rigaud. To himself he says, oh, not René, not her, not now.

Of course it is René.

"I can come by to see you either tonight or tomorrow," she says. "I don't have to pay an extra cent if I go home via Paris. I can come to Gif for a day or two. The weekend. I don't have to be at Yale until Monday night, maybe even not until Tuesday night. It won't cost me anything extra. Do you want me? Do you want to see me?"

"Of course I want you. Come tomorrow. When?"

"A flight arrives at Charles de Gaulle at 10 tomorrow—Friday—unless you want me to come in at 9:30 tonight. I'll probably make it if I leave right now. Both Lufthansa."

"No, don't try to come tonight. It is too late. I won't even be in Paris. I'll be here. I'm working. Come tomorrow. I'll fetch you at Lufthansa arrivals, Charles de Gaulle; recover your valise first. Tomorrow morning at 10. I have to go now. I'm very busy. Please, don't call me here."

"Sorry. See you tomorrow, I can't wait."

Her plane lands promptly at 10. She arrives weighted down, three bags. She hefts her suitcases off the moving luggage belt, one too-large, too-blue American Tourister and its smaller mate. She scans the faces for the quick slim brown-haired, dark-eyed figure with the scar, the sagging round shoulders. He is not there.

Now seated on a round black aluminum-trimmed bench surrounded by suitcases, she peruses the abstract program of the Wiesbaden meeting. Titles draw her attention. "Sources and sinks of atmospheric methane." "Nitrogen oxides of the lower atmosphere." "Interactions between sulphur-containing compounds in the stratosphere." "Tropospheric particulates, carbonate-bicarbonate, and carbon dioxide in freshwater systems." "Gas exchange at the ocean surface." But the same titles, so compelling ten days earlier when they lunched at a phony English teagarden off Sonnenberger Strasse, now were boring. She sniffed the book of abstracts open on her knees. It smelled stale. Where is he? Doesn't he have feelings? How could he not come? She pulls herself to her feet, drags the large bag, lifts her shoulder bag strap across her head, pushes the small matched suitcase and makes her way toward the ladies room. She spots the "consigne" sign. Doesn't that mean "storage cabinet" or "left luggage" or "locker" or something? Still weighted, slow-moving with the shoulder bag burden and kicked smaller valise, she returns to the round bench. Grateful for the one last seat, she squeezes in between a beautiful reddish-blond jetsetter with a matching cocker spaniel and a corpulent Nigerian in his colorful igbada, forehead expanding to a high-domed cap. She views the diamond-studded watch of the blond lady with the shock of alarm. Now 11:20, my God, he's nearly an hour and a half late. Ominous, his absence. What now?

She lugs her bags toward the "Consigne" sign. Embarrassed by her mispronounced monosyllables, she attempts French, camouflaged by mumble. She finally has enough coins to open a bottom portal. She kicks in her suitcases angrily, at last free of these burdens. No choice left but the next move, the inevitable telephone hassle. His numbers and extension written last week in Germany are still there on the abstract program. Is it a local or long-distance call to

Gif-sur-Yvette? She tries French. The *telephoniste* answers her in impeccable English. He makes it clear that outside telephone lines require familiarity. She sits at a counter encircled by Stonehenge-like telephone cabins, each bright orange door numbered one to twelve in black. She copies Raoul's ten-digit number and hands it to the snickering clerk. Inside the cabin the phone rings. Piercingly. Why louder than the others? "*Allo, allo. Extension quoi?*" Again: "*extension quoi?*" She blurts "*deux-deux*" sounding to herself like an idiot mute. Apparently she is understood. She finally hears, after burbling, static and ringing noises and interminable silence, she hears her own voice. "Dr. Gautier?" She is audible. "*Oui, oui, il n'est pas ici maintenant, Mademoiselle,*" sounds like a young man.

When is he going to return?

Not clear, but soon since he left his glasses and jacket on his desk. Won't leave the Gif Institute for long without them; "*lunette,*" "*bureau,*" she thinks, she understands. *Merci*, she says, and hangs up. Now what?

Back to the black bench, out with the abstracts, and her half-written manuscript: "Methane release from ten freshwater sources in the Northeastern U.S." Thirty incoherent pages of scrawl, scientifically too loose, and stylistically clumsy. She recoils at the severity of her self-criticism. She squirms on the only thing that at this moment seems familiar and stable: the long black aluminum-trimmed bench of airportsville in the Old World.

A bright option: she should refuse to wait any longer, change her reservation, leave for New York on the 2 o'clock flight, and be home in Connecticut for supper. How greedy to hope for continuous ecstacy. Why expect togetherness to last? How long had any even minimal affection lasted with Howard? Two months? Aah, men. It was only after Howard that René learned to sublimate passion through the compulsion of chemistry. She had immersed herself in work. She has become one of a very few women taken seriously by Establishment atmospheric chemists. Her scientific self-image is strong and happy. She lives in the camaraderie of colleagues, not in the shadow of a ruling man.

Raoul doesn't waste time with me, she tells herself. I help him work. Why is he rude? Does every love require misery? Every ecstasy an anguish? Ignoring hunger, fatigue, the teeming airport, the flopping flight number boards, she begins to write with the single-mindedness of science she learned only after the Howard fiasco, the idyllic Chicago days. "Dear Raoul." At that moment the airport lights dim. For her they go out entirely. She mutters, "Dear Raoul. Yes, dammit, Dear Raoul. I address this to you but you'll never see it. I write for myself. Perhaps you can't be open with me but I'll tell it like it happened—to me and maybe even to you."

> This year July lasted longer than any other month. The Rhine Castle at Marksburg, beyond Filsen, was started in the four-teenth century and took two centuries to finish. No lichens on its walls. "Here somewhere," announced the British botanist Mitchell Gregson, "must be coal—or a petroleum refinery. The sulfur dioxide content of the surrounding air is too high for lichens. The other castles here, Stahleck and Pfalz, for example, are covered with lichens— lichens abound here in

Germany, they always thrive if atmospheric sulfur dioxide is below ten parts per million." We lowered our heads to go through passageways, the fourteenth century Rhinelanders must have stood smaller than us. You and I and Dr. Mitchell Gregson—the Englishman who wrote that great book on the microbiology of air—were together. We all stumbled into a room hidden behind a passage from which the other tourists were blocked by a velvet cord. Now a delicious odor reached us. I squinted at lights far off and uncertain. I saw rows of candles. The glow behind the candle lineup explained the odor. A spit, roasting meat over a huge fire! We were the Lord's guests! The Knights' Hall adjoined the fourteenth century kitchen. A medieval feast was set. This was the surprise they had referred to—I hadn't any idea, nor did the other scientists realize that at Marksburg Castle, three-and-a-half hours down the Rhine from where the boat had left Biebrich just south of Wiesbaden, we'd be so entertained.

I couldn't keep my eyes off your scarred face. You twinkle-eyed, small, intense man with the scar. We had passed the Loreleifelsen, the legend of someone, not quite a Siren. We embarked at Biebrich, the Rhine port town, suburb of Wiesbaden, with our German hosts led by the neat, trim spokeswoman Mrs. Brunger. We all obediently followed her. "We must have a drink," she announced, "while we await the boat." In that tourist square beneath a tower, the patio, surrounded by small flags from all countries. Boy Scouts queued up to enter a ski lift through the tower. Gay colors, khakis and neckerchiefs. A young, pretty woman next to me introduced herself as Mrs. Taumann, who wanted to practice English.

"Yes, my husband and I had our happiest days in California,

San Jose. Americans speak frankly. You can send the children out to play. You can tell American neighbors your feelings. You all have capacitisch freezers so you only need go to market twice a week. My children were at school all day so I worked a bit and studied English. My good American friends still send us Christmas cards."

Mrs. Taumann said the next in a hushed voice. "I lost my husband, you know, just three months ago. He was only forty-four. He had worked for Dr. Brunger for years, second in charge of our Max Planck Institute." She clung now to the white-haired, cool Mrs. Brunger who has grown old with dignity and beauty, the way I hope I will grow old.

"In Germany, here I mean, life is different," continued Mrs. Taumann. "I'm working now. They all told me to take it slowly, to work no more than twice a week. I never worked while I was married, of course not. But I have been lucky. I mean, even though he died young and left me with two children, the Max Planck Institute is like a family, my family. They have all taken care of me. They knew my husband very well of course. They have given me a partial job. It must be difficult for you to believe, but there are very few such jobs in all of Germany. What do you say? Half-time? Part-time? These jobs are very few, here. Married women don't work. It's changing, I guess, but slowly. The Institute here has wonderful people. I've been lucky," she sighed, "but I miss the U.S."

Mrs. Brunger nodded at me, "You must drink, girl," she said in a motherly, definite way, and looked, dismayed, at the left half of the table—where all seven atmosphericists and their guests had slipped into German.

"I apologize for my countrymen. They are not comfortable

with English. They have not, like us, me and Mrs. Taumann here, lived in the States. We lived there in Lexington, Massachusetts, near Boston, for four years. Do you know it? My husband worked in Bedford, at the Armed Forces Atmosphere Research Laboratory. Some of our best years were there in New England, as you probably—but my goodness, the boat may leave without us—we must get down to the dock!"

We all followed Mrs. Brunger again. Her neat white hair tied in the back in a bun helped lead us in single file down to the boat. Our international meeting honored her husband: Klaus Brunger, a jolly, sparkling man articulate in American English. His institute was leader in measurements of air. He retires this year. Over twenty years ago Brunger discovered many compounds in the atmosphere; terpenes, nitrous oxide. Before others, he realized that these gases, compounds, and structures, even "formed elements" like pollen, tiny seeds, and fungal spores, come from life.

The meeting was organized by Brunger's colleague, Werner Zeiloff, who in my opinion wisely titled it, "The Biological Contribution to the Atmosphere." Zeiloff, I think, founded a field of science by his choice of words. As Darly-James had told me, after his Yale seminar last year, the gases are kept in place by the incessant breathing and farting of microbes, animals, and plants. The atmospheric scientists don't know that yet. They say life passively adapts and therefore is irrelevant. Zeiloff, an original, is only just beginning to see. I wanted to meet him. I recognized him from photos. Meteorologists mentioned stratospheric balloons and the influence of plants on clouds. Chromatographers talked about columns. Nitrogen on

Mars was compared with Earth and Venus. I think, anyway I hope, I was invited not just because I was a woman (the program does have three women) but because of my own work. I published support for Brünger's ideas that life makes gas. I'm probably a Brunger disciple. The first morning Zeiloff reviewed the oxides of carbon: measured in a box. Up in light, down in dark—if plants were in there. Plants were crucial. Zeiloff, a chemist, notices that microbes and plants speed up nature's chemistry. The American Donald Peterson took hundreds of samples of ocean air—he idolizes Brunger.

Peterson followed most closely behind Mrs. Brunger. She led us from our drinks on the hill down the brick-paved, flower-box-lined stony street to the dock. I stayed behind as our scientist crowd ascended the large Rhine boat. An announcement I barely understood was in British English. They said something about a special dining room assigned to our International Atmospheric Congress. The broad-faced, big-chested lady in her blue uniform and wide blue skirt announced, "Note, please, members of the international atmosphere congress descend please to B4, mind the step, mind your head." International? Not really very international. Among our white-badged group I heard a Dutch accent, but the blond man had "Boulder, Colorado" on his name badge. Charles Van Warden. Yes, he had come from Holland years ago as a boy. Only Americans, Germans, and a few Englishmen. Hardly international. Nearly the entire crowd of two hundred atmosphere people squeezed down one by one to the B4 deck. I took my time and monitored the flow. The few exceptions I could see to the usual white Anglo-Saxon-Protestant-scientist types were the German wives, most wearing crosses.

I knew Van Warden only by mail and telephone, I know he's a member of the Atmosphere Establishment. He's head of the National Center for Atmospheric Research–NCAR? No. NOAA? NOAA—what is it? National Oceanic and Atmospheric Administration, USA? Before this meeting, some eighteen months ago, I wrote him to ask if I could do research in his lab. Friends told me Van Warden let his people follow their own scientific instincts. Van Warden wrote that his positions involve deployment of heavy equipment into the field. It was a way to tell me that he is reluctant to employ women, I don't think any of his post-docs or good students have been women. (The proof is in the pudding.) His letter made me dislike him. He also wrote that I did work "out-of-his-field" that therefore he "couldn't judge."

I was excited by the fact that the important Van Warden—I even managed to speak to him once after penetrating a baffle of secretaries—stood only five feet away from me on the sunny Rhineland boat dock. I felt bold when I said: "You are Van Warden." "Yes." Pause. I asked him about Will Kellogg, his co-author. Kellogg, the summer I was a National Science Foundation fellow, was my horny boss. I said, "Is our mutual friend Kellogg still married to his wife?" Van Warden shook and became icy. "I do not talk about the private lives of my friends." OK, no shit, I thought and smiled. So much for an NCAR or NOAA job for me.

I filed slowly into the dining room, nearly everyone already seated at tables of eight, Van Warden near me at a table of seven with a conspicuous hole for a single. A gray-bearded German colleague motioned to me to join. Just then I spied you. You, scarred-face Frenchman, were right there at the next, but full, table. I mumbled, "Hoping to have a French lesson." Gautier, you didn't understand me until I repeated myself again very clearly. You said, "No one here speaks my languages, not even French." I knew you meant science language. "Come here." You said it so definitely in a tone that ordered me to follow. You got up, and left the table of eight.

I followed to the dark far edge of the group. The Ionescus, Romanians, sat alone there with six empty chairs. For the next two days we smiled at beautiful Mrs. Ionescu and her large-eared husband. We never had any languages in common. "Deutsch?" they asked. "Nein. English?" "No," they responded. "Français?" "Non," sadly. "Espagnole? Italiano?" "Nein," they answered, "Russki?" We shook our heads. We never spoke again. Although I passed the graduate exam, even my German is poor. Yours is worse! They became our mute witnesses.

You were patient with me, Raoul, and my stilted French. You explained: Lorelei called out from high on the steep banks, she seduced all passersby. I still don't understand the difference between Lorelei and the Sirens. You said something about hiding vineyards, invasions from the banks, downstream migration, castle forts. Alternation of Franco-German masters over the centuries, European chess games. You reverted to English each time I looked bewildered. Steve Ramsey's hawk-nosed post-doc walked past: "You may not be learning atmospheric chemistry techniques straight from the horse's mouth," he teased, "but your French is certainly improving!"

Our crowd of scientists finally disembarked onto buses and then toward Marksburg Castle. We started on the steep rocky path, others followed the paved road. "Verboten!" cried an alarmed Castle guide. "Interdit," you and I exclaimed gleefully.

Like sheep we grouped for the tour and you surveyed me. Why did our guide speak English so fluently? He was a secondary school history teacher, an Ulsterman, who talked liltingly of his exile. He led us to the massive, carved, iron-studded castle doors. You chose the English-speaking group to avoid the Germans. I wanted even then to believe that you joined Ulsterman because of me.

He led us through winding passageways, low ceilings, a tunnel, to a fourteenth century chapel. Ancient Rhinelanders in their last minutes prayed to an unreliable God for protection from enemies. You were too tall for the chapel ceiling, I fit perfectly. Most of the gawky Germans and Americans bent over as they entered. Even most of the blond wives were too tall. Dungeon chairs, thumbscrews, ankle cuffs, and rusty chains on exhibit. I told you then that I'm from Saskatoon, Saskatchewan, a province you'd never heard of with names you couldn't spell.

With perhaps 180 others, still single file, we entered the windowless chamber, attracted by delicious odor and crackling noises. A huge fire spilled light on the long narrow tables, rows of Rhine wine bottles, the pageant staged for us: The Knights' Hall of the Castle. Two stocky attendants dressed in doublet and hose rotated enormous spit handles. Dr. Klaus Brunger and his frau, formally dressed in matching black suits, bow ties, and white blouses, like permanently mated penguins that glowed in firelight. They wore their lifetime of devotion on their breasts. I looked at you speaking science to our American colleagues. You are missing teeth on your scarred left side. I felt euphorique. (Is that the word?) Your talk gyrated from volatiles of air and sea through vapors and aromas of wines. I couldn't eat and became silent. You put on your reading glasses and read the bottle labels.

I spoke quietly to the gentleman on my left, Heinrich D. Holland, about marine geochemistry and the ocean-atmosphere system. I recognized his name, I even knew they call him Dick. I admire his German fluency and expertise. I had bought his textbook a week before I met you. I felt reticent. This Harvard man reviews grant proposals for the National Science Foundation, he will probably see mine. The impression I make on him may affect my research support. Holland told me that his family "had been Jewish but it wasn't any more." I knew, everyone knew, that he was born and had lived in Germany until the age of twelve. His trace of a German accent surfaces only when he's excited.

Steve Ramsey told his post-doc who told me that Professor H. D. Holland had been a fundamentalist Christian in college. "What are you now?" I asked him. He chose his words with care and evaded a straight answer. His Christian stage, he admitted, was when he worked with Ramsey. An aberrant epoch, brought on from exhaustion from the burden of being Jewish. When Holland stops worrying about his "zehr correctness" and talks science, as on that night, he amazes me. He described an expedition to Iceland, the geochemical activity at the mid-Atlantic ridge. He showed me wallet-size photos of pillow basalt, drawn out hastily from his passport holder. The shockingly hot activity was aligned nearly straight north to south. These rocks look like their name: "pillows" of lava. I mentioned my colleague David's experiments—that he measured methane gas collected from these very rift zones, probably from the same samples. I told Professor Holland that I should have studied geology instead of chemistry. Chemists are stuck in labs whereas geologists travel.

The guests leaned back in their chairs, relaxed, many smoking, when I went outside, to see that the fresh air of dusk had turned to night. I thought, now or never. Was I brave enough to show my attraction to you? I closed my eyes only to see the smooth tracery of your scar.

We rode together on the return bus, Raoul. I don't remember leaving the warm dining chamber. I mentioned that I planned to visit my brother in Munich right after this meeting. I had said he was there "on holiday" because you didn't understand me when I said "on vacation."

You asked me about bacterial gas emission in the marsh. Methane, ammonia, nitrogen. We spoke about paleoatmospheres, Brunger's contribution—he moved the discussion into the realm of polite scientific society. Why does everyone agree that oxygen in the Earth's atmosphere is produced by living beings whereas all the other reactive gases (nitrogen, methane, carbon dioxide, ammonia) are just chemicals or volcanic emissions?

Then you told me that your grandmother died and you were with her. I could not believe it when you said you had never married. Actually my heart stopped when you told me that.

Why did your disclosure affect me so? Why was I elated? What are you, you brown-eyed, scar-faced man, what are you to me?

You ruffled my hair as I watched the great Rhine River, a black ribbon stretching along the bus route on that black velvet night. We were quiet, exciting quiet. You felt it too, I know. We got off the bus at the Wiesbaden Spa Hotel. Do you know that

I was in pain, emotional pain, when we went out for drinks on the street with your American colleagues? All of them seemed ridiculous to me that night. Banal Don Peterson, fast-talking Alton Brainerd, friendly and funny Steve Ramsey.

Peterson challenged us to join him at a porno show, the "entertainment lounge" of gaudy painted girlies, black net hose, and flowered garters. I offered to go only because I hoped you would come with us, but you refused. The invitation died. The conversation degenerated into old-times stuff. You four had been together at the Coastal Upwelling Ecosystems Analysis meetings. All of you were members of the oxygen and carbon gas study section. You sounded silly speaking American, the talky talky pained me. You bought my glass of wine but not theirs. After we all trekked back to the Spa Hotel, I watched you say good-bye to them and ascended my four flights of stairs. I couldn't sleep after that exhilarating time. I realized at that moment, R. Gautier, you scar-faced man, I didn't even know your first name!

You weren't at breakfast. Alton Brainerd told me you that are seldom very late but you are never on time. During the lecture Steve Ramsey, nearsighted with contact lenses, sat between us in the front row. We (you, me, and Ramsey) all wanted to be close to the action. I wrote you my first "lettre"—to ask your name and room number. I crossed out my question. You answered, correcting my French because I asked you to. That little slip of paper was lesson one. You wrote that you hadn't slept well. I concluded that the feelings were there. From that our first epistolary moment, you have matched my verbosity with hesitation.

I concentrated hard: I disagreed with much of Brainerd's

work on nitrous oxide. When would these chemists wake up and realize the power of bacteria to force the chemically unlikely to occur? Next. Ehhalt's summary of global cycles of methane: could methane control the oxygen? Here, listening to Ehhalt's talk and Zeiloff's questions, I suggested that methane, produced in the absence of oxygen, may influence oxygen. I pushed past you on my way to the ladies' room, and dropped you another note. Unabashed, I asked you: Are you going to Nachenheim? Are you going to see the Guttenberg Bible? "A ce soir," you answered.

As dusk, the sessions over, we joined the milling group in the rain in front of the hotel. You didn't walk or sit with me when the huge group toured Nachenheim—the inevitable bus to the inevitable wine cellar. Filled with round tables, flowered tablecloths, the cellar looked like Hollywood. The German master of ceremonies became louder and, we suspected, bawdier, judging from the groans and laughter.

The rain stopped. Yearning for air, moon, and stars, I went upstairs and outside. I walked along the trellis as I approached our parked bus. I knew you too would have to walk through the garden, but you didn't come to find me as I hoped you would. The laughing company ambled upstairs also readying to leave. Smiling, wrinkling your scar, you passed with your independent air through the garden and said slowly, "C'est très frais ce soir." As we arrived and you passed by my bus seat, you quickly invited me to walk to Brunnenkolannade, to the Kirkviertel around the Kirkhaus on Wilhelmstrasse to seek the ancient Roman baths. Please don't invite your atmosphere-monitoring American friends to go with us, I thought but did not say.

We planned to walk to the thermal fountain. But we kept on. What was your room number? We trudged to the fifth floor and you opened the door to gently pull me toward you. We never saw the Brunnenkolannade, whatever that is, nor the Kirkpark, the Kirkviertel, or any Roman baths. You turned off time, your solid-state travel clock read 00000. Forty-six years old and never any wife. I figure that you must have turned time off for many women before me.

Where are you? Why haven't you come to the airport for me? Is it all over?

René shakes her hand, cramped from writing, signs "Love" and becomes aware that the lights have again turned on at Charles de Gaulle. Crowds, all unrecognized faces, bob in the Lufthansa waiting area. The time is now 3:45. She suspects her scribbling is drivel, but it certainly has been therapeutic. She asks herself again, what kind of man is he?

She checks two clocks and a watch to verify the hour. Since her plane arrived on time at 10 o'clock she has been here. She approaches a new *telephoniste*. Cubicle number one. Why does she worry so? Why is she so incompetent in this melodious language?

"Gautier?"

"*Oui, ici, Gautier.*"

"René."

"Oh, it is you! Where are you?"

"Where do you think I am? Charles de Gaulle."

"For so long? Why?"

"Why didn't you come for me?"

"Well, I planned to . . . indeed I tried, I left in the direction of Charles de Gaulle. Traffic was terrible, worse than usual. I realized to fetch you was hopeless, I went back to the lab. Why don't you call me before now?"

"I did."

"That is not possible. I am here all day."

"Forget it, Gautier. I'll come to Gif right now—I just need to get the train at Denfert-Rochereau. I know how."

"No, no, no—don't do that. Positively not. I'm too busy. They'll all talk. Don't come now. I'll meet you tonight at the Gare du Nord. Do you know it?"

"Yes. Should I bring my luggage?"

"Of course. Take a cab. Bring your valise to the Gare du Nord. I'll see you at the station café after work—tonight at nine."

He does not wait, the phone clicks with finality.

What now is she to do for the next five hours? She retrieves her American suitcases from the *consigne*. She alights the bus to Paris Air Terminal to make her way to a second *consigne*. Her bags stowed, Metro map in hand, she frees herself and emerges into the oblique sunlight of late summer in Paris. From Les Invalides, across the expanse she gazes at the gorgeous Pont Alexandre III. She admires the Eglise du Dome. The seventeenth-century Hardouin Mansart had outdone himself in splendor: golden dome of golden domes across river of rivers, past bridge of bridges. She nibbles left-over Lufthansa tidbits. An hour later, luggage dragging, she seeks the Gare du Nord. Direction Chateau de Vincennes to Strasbourg St. Denis. Direction Ponte de Clignancourt, three stops to Gare du Nord. She does not permit the luxury of a taxi. Even if she manages to say "Gare du Nord," how will she understand the driver's answer? She mastered the Metro before. The huge blue bag becomes the object of curious stares, the lugging particularly painful at the Metro steps and the *correspondances* (transfer points). Tired and hungry, she arrives at the dim station, drags up the escalator, across the great expanse from Metro to actual Gare.

The black-handed foggy clock unmistakably marks 9:15. A corner window displays an alarm clock and a pocket watch, digitally they read 21:17. The station is hot and sour. She scans serious commuters, groups of Scandinavian students, Scottish backpackers, sleeping vacationing families, children, and dogs and realizes that, now, she needs the public toilet. Are the two pinch-faced bavard women who collect two-franc pieces legitimate? Raoul, you bastard, why do you do this to me?

Relieved again of luggage in still another *consigne* she reconnoiters. No Gautier. 9:30 and 9:32. Which "café?" Labeled "bar," a corner place serves fast food American style at sit-down tables. On the far side a stand-up bar has liquor. The restaurant on the mezzanine is *fermé*. Which café? Back to the Metro station, back to the rails. She climbs again the stairway to the closed restaurant. Then back to the money-changing booth. Why are the impatient people queued up at the currency exchange at this late hour all Anglo-Saxon; that is, English-speaking and nearly all blond. Is money Anglo-Saxon?

Gautier, why torture me? Do you punish me for giving you pleasure? Do you resent our intimacy? Has an accident, a crisis, a death in the family, something horrible, some nameless detention occurred? Where are you?

René's hunger changes from intermittent to steady; determined to conquer her fear of speaking she must ask for something to eat.

By the time he arrives at 10:15, her eagerness and sense of urgency are transformed to indifference. She had rehearsed various opening phrases of frustration and regret. Not hungry anymore and coffee-awake, she spots him from her square table. She feels it: the forgiveness flows outward. She masks both her initial elation followed nearly immediately by bitter disappointment.

"I was at the other café," he says feebly as he slips into a chair beside her.

"You were not! When?"

"A while ago."

"You have not been in the Gare du Nord for more than five minutes. You know that and so do I."

"Well, I was working. The cruise is next week. Every damn screw has to be in place before we sail. It is difficult." He looks ambivalent. "Where do you stay tonight?"

"What do you mean?"

"Where do you stay? Which hotel?"

"I thought I was staying with you."

"You can't. My flat's too small."

"You are nuts. You never told me to take a hotel. I . . ." She holds back tears.

"OK, just for tonight, but never again. If you ever come again to Paris, you take a hotel. You can stay tonight because it is late. Tomorrow we find an hotel."

"Raoul, don't you know what I feel for you? What do you mean, if I ever 'come again to Paris'?" Her voice distressed.

"Don't you feel *l'amour, le vrai amour*?" he teases, smiling now. "Come on, let's get your valise."

She knots both his hands and with determination forces him to look at her. "Please, you don't understand. What do I care if your apartment is small? Only your not showing up bothers me. I want us to be together like in Wiesbaden."

He looks embarrassed. "Come, let's fetch your things and go. I have too much to do."

His flat is minuscule and nearly empty except for a few elegant objects. Radio, phonograph, and built-in digital clock, complete Bach cantatas, romantic and baroque records. One teapot, two cups, two wine glasses, two beer mugs, one short-handled broom, one large bed, all in the narrow high-ceilinged room. A tiny bathroom; a miniature sink, the "water," and the smallest, most un-American bathtub René has ever seen. A seat not a tub, one sits up straight while spattering oneself with water from the hose. Through the window are the mansards over the Place Dauphine, garrets of western culture. The only entrance to his tower is a six-flight tramp up winding stairs.

The Algerian boy at street level is concièrge. He hides in a tiny roomlet to the right of an impressive cast-iron gate at the door facing the famous street. The street spews images: not ten yards from the spot on which, seventy-one years before, Louis Manin's cart horse crushed the depressed Nobel laureate Pierre Curie to death. Pont-Neuf, rue Dauphine, René notes, has scientific connections. Didn't George Sand (née Aurore Dupin) write novels here? There is more history on this tiny street than in the whole province of

Saskatchewan. Gautier is impressed that this Canadian prairie girl knows Pierre Curie attempted to cross *rue Dauphine* in the rain.

She shares his bed. They sleep. He insists, first up, Saturday morning that he go to register her, on her credit card, at a walking-distance hotel near the Theatre Odéon. He leaves only to return in less than a quarter hour to hand her the registration receipt and an admonishment that she park there at least her smaller valise. Then he leaves, summarily, not even a good-bye. Unaccustomed to the luxury of time, she pulls out the program, the reprints, her notes from Wiesbaden and immerses herself in the writing of the money-justifying meeting report, due in New Haven next Wednesday. Startled from the nearly finished first draft of the report by hunger, she seeks relief. Dry almonds, peanuts, dates, and wedges of La Vâche Qui Ris nicely suffice. By dusk the second draft begins to look coherent. At 23:20 he tries not to disturb her: stretched on the bed face down, lights ablaze, she has fallen asleep on many papers. He gently tries to coax her to tidy them up, now, and leave his cubby home at Place Dauphine. That night he admonishes her to take her baggage and insists she leave the Place Dauphine flat. She murmurs, dreaming, perhaps defiant. In spite of himself he falls asleep beside her. He awakes at 6:30 and attempts to force her out. "Up, *vite, vite*. Get up."

"Why? Why move when this is the best joy of life?"

"What do you think we are doing? Up now, young lady. Go back to your hotel. Now! I'm late, I'm very late. I should be to Gif by now."

"Now? But it's Sunday."

"So?"

"Come on, Raoul, climb back in here."

"Get up and out, young lady. Out, out, out! Enough foolishness. Now! I've a thousand things to do. The cruise leaves next Saturday. Do you think the equipment can be ready without me?"

"Why does an hour or two on a Sunday morning matter?"

No answer.

"Gautier, answer me."

"If I answer you, you won't be happy. I must be at Gif at ten, lock the door when you go. *Tu m'agace*."

That is all.

What to do? Sunday. Where to go? The same problem. Perhaps she will take the bus to Charles de Gaulle, make a new reservation, cancel her Monday afternoon flight, and go home now. The thought of returning to the de Gaulle airport depresses her. He never tells her when he is coming, where he is going. She had asked him, "Why do you measure the sulfur dioxide and dimethyl sulfoxide?"

"Why?" he had answered, annoyed. "What do you mean, why? Why do I measure gases?"

"Why, yes, why do you make these measurements? What do you want to know? How does it help?"

"For Chrissake—*merde*!" he had finally answered. "Do I have to listen to you about my measurements, too? I don't have enough of this all day? I'll be back," he had said, and left the flat. That was about 7 a.m., 7:12 to be exact on Sunday morning: she could see it on bright orange decimals of the stereo set clock. She even noted it in her diary: 7:12. When he returned the clock read 22:05:48. She hears him mount the stairs, of course, fuss at the lock, open the door wide. He stares at her in surprise.

"Who gave you a key to this place? Did I? No, of course I didn't."

"No, of course you didn't; you'd never give me a key. I just never locked the door. I only left for little while to wander around the Quarter."

"Why? Why do you stay? Why didn't you go back to your hotel?"

"Why, Raoul, because I want to make love with you."

"Go back to your hotel. I need sleep. I don't feel well."

"When are we going to talk about the sulfur gases?"

No answer. A slight smile.

"When are you going to tell me why and how you measure sulfides and dimethyl sulfoxide? Where did you go? Why did you come back so late? Why don't you tell me anything? Why don't you do what you say you'll do?"

"Leave, please," he says, kissing her lightly. She grabs at him passionately to kiss him the way she feels. His reserve makes her awkward.

"Go away. You're too young. It's too late. I can't lie around all night."

He tries to persuade her to go to her hotel. She refuses. In the end, again, he lets her stay. He sleeps well. She lies awake, wondering why she feels so foreign, why she is still there. Friends say the French are obsessed with privacy—they seldom permit any strangers into their homes. They must not be judged by Canadian standards.

Doesn't he care? Does he care? Should she abandon her post-doc program at Yale, her adjunct assistant professorship, to try for a NATO exchange fellowship in France? If he has never before found the closeness that she offers, surely he won't find it now? She, twenty-seven years old, and open to love, yes. He, already in his mid-forties, closed, withdrawn, alone, no? They can do so many beautiful things together. They have so much to share with each other. He needed her in Wiesbaden. But Wiesbaden is over.

"How did you get your scar?" she had asked in Wiesbaden on their second night together. She gently ran her fingers down his scar from the top of the nose nearly to his chin. He batted her hand away roughly.

"During the war."

"How did you get it?"

"Just wartime."

"Tell me please, I want to know. It's not just curiosity. I want to know all about you."

"Go to sleep," he said. "This is Germany. I told you already that I can't tell you about the war while we are in Germany. I'll tell you at home, in Paris."

And last night were they not home in Paris? She asked again, "How did you get your scar?" And he answered, "Go to sleep. Leave me alone, *laisse moi.* Sh! Sh! Sh! *Du calme.*" Will she ever know this man?

She decides: she must go home now. Right now. She will write him long letters. Her French will improve. The GEOSECS III meetings a year from October are soon enough. She will wait for him. Working furiously she will offer up her best work to him and his colleagues. He will delight in her honesty, the thoroughness of her methane study. She will labor with him at his pace and at his level, excite and support him. A year? What is a single year if they share the next twenty? A year is short in the training of a scientist. Time enough to learn the language of the field, but not enough time to solve any of its problems. Not long enough to determine whether research (upper atmospheric physics, recombination reactions of the stratosphere, design of new chromatographs) or teaching (freshman chemistry, analytical chemistry) is your first option. A year in the reckoning of the world, however, is time enough to make a sure decision. Perhaps just long enough.

She collects her things, packs up her handbag with the shoulder strap. She will have to return to Place d'Odéon before 9 in the morning to pick up her lesser blue valise, to be sure to make the early afternoon flight. How small his flat is; Raoul's description did not exaggerate. She does not know him. The small cupboard and the counterboard above the tucked-in refrigerator in the minuscule kitchen are bare. Does he ever eat here? Does he drink coffee? How can he ever cook? Where does he eat? No table, the cluttered desk top is too tiny to service even one. Does he have a housekeeper? If she is fat, René chuckles, she can't even turn around in this kitchen. Does he bring women here, she thinks, only to relieve himself of sperm when his mood strikes? She knows his scientific papers and his gas-sampling techniques far better than she knows the man himself.

Does he have lovers? A mistress? She tells herself not to care. She can't be jealous when she knows no mistress could possibly share the gases, the inner sanctum of his life. By 7:30 Monday morning he has gone. Again, without explanation he has left her to her own devices, to return, herself, to Charles de Gaulle, valises and all. "Please be sure both upstairs and downstairs doors lock properly," was all he said.

At 8:30 she closes his door. She lets the small blue valise drag and descends the six flights of stairs. Her spirits rise with every step. Paris in August. Paris, the Latin Quarter—a Parisian lover, a colleague. Now, René, what else do you want? Soon it will be next year, 1978, and the third meeting of the atmospheric subcommittee of GEOSECS. September, soon, in Providence, Rhode Island.

Sept. 10, 1977

Dear Raoul:

I came home exhausted, of course. I now have a parakeet whom I wanted to name Volatile or Psittacosis—but I've settled on Methyl (she is female). My officemate (David, the one from Iowa) promised to be a very industrious birdkeeper when I go away next week. Methyl looks well: some good greens and mostly blue, fluffy feathers. I still wake up at about three in the morning ready to work and fall asleep immediately after supper. I still have my arm across the bed to feel for you—I became accustomed to you so quickly. I reach, while half-asleep, for your scar, I run my hand down your nose, to your neck and farther down, down, down, marking your finest edges. Then I wake up with a start: you are not here. Too much distance between us. Why do we allow age, time, and space to separate us so severely? Do you ever even think about me?

I leave for class in 15 minutes. I must finish the lake manuscript, meet David in the lab at 10:30, go to see Lerner, my older boss who goes tomorrow to Washington. A million things to do. I'd much rather sit here writing to you as a last dawn of summer peeks in my window.

Please do take care of yourself.

And please, read this John Donne sonnet I've enclosed. . . . It expresses far better than I can how I feel toward you. "Sir, more than kisses letters mingle soules." No?

And please please write.

And please, do send me a copy of the annual report of your Institute . . . the green-covered one that I was reading just before I left. I need some of the references in it soon for the manuscript I'm working on.

Je t'aime,

René

September 30, 1977

Dear René,

I love you so strong. Very strong, I need you, to kiss you deeply. I love that you are sparkling with life, with intelligence. With regard to your letters I was sad because it seemed to me that your love declined very fast, unfaithful woman, declined exponentially.

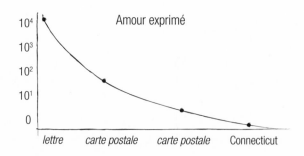

But now today I received your letter with the poem. I know Shakespeare sonnet, even in English, but not John Donne. This reassured me some. I have a great desire to write you a long erotic letter but I don't dare. I want to talk to you about science in English because in French I never do it proper. I want to talk about the nitrogen gases: nitrous oxides, nitrogen, ammonia and their cycles and the chemistry and biology of all of them. We won't understand the air unless we consider all these fields: geology, biology, chemistry, atmospheric science, meteorology, and climatology. Atmospheres do not obey the laws of borders. They diffuse across all artificial barriers just as we must let our minds do, and as you and I let our bodies do. I love you altogether: as one whole. I yearn to embrace you. I hope you have a good memory of the dusk and the dawn at the Place Dauphine and all that happened in between! But, I am, I'm afraid, "un français trop vieux." It is too late for me to send, on time for your paper, the annual report. I won't have a copy for three weeks. Even worse, I'm not sure that I come to GEOSECS next September in Rhode Island because Leysson may not let me. So much the worse. I love you.
Raoul

October 2, 1977
Dear Raoul,

Why don't you answer me? I've sent five letters in two weeks to Gif. And you don't respond. I rush to my mailbox every day, waiting, wishing, hoping, that I mean as much to you as you mean to me.

What do you measure these days? At least tell me that. I won't waste your time. I love you so. Probably our love is far less permanent than the landscape, and the intensity I feel is likely to have been exacerbated by the thousands of miles between us. Anyway, there it is.

Love,

René

October 12, 1977

Dear Raoul,

I've written you ten letters but vowed—vowed not to send a single one until I heard from you. I will not permit you or myself such indulgence. If you don't send for them—and, by the way, write me a real letter—I'll burn them all.

I hope your work goes well.

René

November 2, 1977

Ma très chère René,

Don't be sad. Send me your pile of letters. Be well. We will see each other again sometime—who knows when? Be happy. I love you and I kiss you strong (hard??). I'm working.

Raoul

December 4, 1977

Dear Raoul,

Before I met you I couldn't talk to anyone in a sincere and open way. Was it the same for you? You come from a more sophisticated environment. Did you have friends or colleagues? Of course now I have colleagues with whom I have no problem talking about straight science. But to talk about everything and to hug at the same time! Wow!! Raoul, I miss you. I just got your September 30th letter today! Did you forget to mail it—when you know I am frantic to hear from you?

Please come to GEOSECS III. Tell Leysson I said so! If you don't tell him I'll call him and insist, I swear. I can't wait until September.

Stay well. Write soon.

Love,

René

January 5, 1978

Dear René,

I respect you very much as well as love you. Your letters are "adorable." I love you very much even if it doesn't seem like it. I just need the fact that you exist. I will tell you when the date will be fixed for my journey next fall to the USA. Above all, be well. I still love you. Of course. Yes. The lettre of septembre was in my nitrous oxide archive since a very long time. Pardon me!

Raoul

April 31, 1978

Dear Raoul,

J. E. Tolly, Jr. (my younger boss) and Professor Lerner called me in today. They both reviewed the paper David and I wrote on the methane production. They asked to speak to both of us—David and me together. I knew something was up. I had written the paper: terse but to the point and loaded with information, especially in the tables. There are definitive cycles, of course, and they plot nicely on a sine curve. Although I wrote the paper, David edited it closely, improved it in a hundred small ways. Of course David gave me all his data, without which it would not have been a paper. So we went together, wondering what Tolly and Lerner wanted. We saw right away. Lerner said first thing that our work was supported by his grant. Tolly said, "Yes, and David is working off another grant which is in my name." I figured it out immediately. They should have just said from the beginning that they wanted their names on our paper. Fair enough. When Lerner had the nerve to "wonder" if he should be first author I nearly agreed, wanted to get out of that office as soon as possible. David Barclay, shy as he may be around the big bosses, then showed them his true colors. "Are you joking?" David asked bluntly. "René planned the experiments, executed them, took the chromatograph into the field, roped me into doing the plate counts, wrote the paper, and now we've submitted it to you. She must be first author. I must be second author. Everything else is fine."

Well, they backed down, the shits. We are adding their names because they provided the money, and they'll need credit for it next time they apply for grants. I'm grateful to David and proud of him. We'll send the paper in very soon. I'm just missing a reference or two, which reminds me, you never did send me the green report from your laboratory. I need that as a reference for this paper, too, and would dearly love to have it soon. You said you would send it months ago, last autumn even. Oh, Raoul, do you ever do what you say you'll do? I keep feeling you will. You must.

Oh, please, next September, come soon. I faint with impatience. Please, Gautier, come to me in September. I can't wait.
Love,
René

June 12, 1978
Dear René,

Thank you for your letters . . . all of them. Of course I love you. You are a marvelous person, an adorable personality. I love you so much. I learn more from you than you do from me, that's sure. You write so well, with such perceptions of life. So

sharp, so strong. I just hope that you will keep me in the fashion that you wish, in your heart. You have profoundly impressed me. I hug you again, as at Place Dauphine, as at Wiesbaden.
Raoul

August 1, 1978
Dear Raoul,

I have many letters for you. I REFUSE TO SEND THEM BECAUSE YOU DON'T ANSWER MINE.
Love,
René

August 25, 1978
Dear René,

Don't please, don't be worried if I do not write you more often. It is because I am older and peut-être a little wise. I don't want to make you crazy with too frequent or too burning letters. And, of course, I am busy as you know. I went last week to Toulouse to use the marvelous microscopic and probe equipment. I thought of you, of us, very much during this trip. I still love you—strongly.

It has been very rainy this August in Paris, but these last few days it has been marvelous. Autumn announces itself, the air at Gif is splendid. I love you but I have other loves too: my work, especially on the sea and the high mountains. Do not be offended. I still want to touch you.

I wrote a paper for the Congress on Aerosols at Galway (Ireland)—it should be longer, it is only five pages. I know the best scientific papers can be short—like yours—but we aren't all geniuses, are we? I send you here abstracts—if you can do it I wish you will send me the new review paper of Steve

Ramsey on carbon and nitrogen cycles that was published in the National Academy of Sciences (or was it the Proc. Royal Society of London?) I think it has the ozone and freon problem in it, no? At Marseille I gave a little communication (one of the abstracts, here it is) showing we know almost nothing about exchange of particles between the atmosphere and the ocean. Much more data are needed on gas exchange. I will see you at the next GEOSECS meeting, Rhode Island—I hope. But for now I still absolutely can't tell you whether Leysson or I (or both of us) shall be going.

Love,

Raoul

The second of September 1978 Gautier stands before his mail-slot in the Institute office. He opens a U.S. airmail red-white-and-blue letter with its stamp of a jet airplane taking off. This letter, he knows, will help firm his plans. He sees the agenda for the next GEOSEC's grantee meeting: University of Rhode Island, 21 and 22 September. How fortuitous: Connecticut and Rhode Island are close together. To himself: I anticipate René's warmth but I am relieved not to have to lose any time. Do I dare admit this to myself? An ugly old guy like me with a beautiful young girl in love with me? She, a scientist, immersed in my work. My gases. I ache to be near her, to smell her hair and whisper to her about our work.

The second page, now ripped through, contains the printed program. Perfect, he notes. All the research directly interests him. The dinner speech, he reads with keen delight, will be delivered by someone Raoul considers to be a really great scientist.

1978 GEOSECS: Atmospheric subgroup

Thursday, Sept. 21

9:00 - 10:00	Nitrogen oxides	Alton Brainerd
10:00 - 11:00	Carbon cycle: CO and CO_2 in the troposphere	Wolfgang Zeiloff
11:00 - 11:30	Sensitivity and error in gas measurements	Donald Peterson
11:30 - 12:00	Geographical aspects of global monitoring of tropospheric gases	Stephen Ramsey
12:00 - 2:00	Lunch	
2:00 - 3:00	Methane and other reduced gases	Dieter Ehhalt J. E. Tolly, Jr. René Pemberlain
3:00 - 4:00	Sulfur cycle: dimethyl sulfide, dimethyl sulfoxide	Charles Van Warden
4:00 - 5:00	Open discussion	
6:00 - 7:00	COCKTAILS	
7:00 - 8:00	DINNER: Whaling Room, Howard Johnson's Motel	
8:00	International Decade of Oceanic Exploration: Toward a Worldwide Data Bank. Do we need an IYGM (International Year of Gas Monitoring?)	Klaus Brunger

Friday, September 22

9:00 - 12:00	Executive Session: Future research and its support (discussion)	All GEOSECS atmospheric subcommittee principal investigators

---

Certainly, decided. I will fly in the 20th, Wednesday night and leave by Sunday the 24th. Quickly now: my note to her must go out with today's mail pick up. Raoul writes in haste, still standing at the mailboxes, one foot on the winding marble staircase, leaning on the bannister.

September 1, 1978

René,

   The GEOSECS meeting schedule looks good for us. I project to arrive on Air France to New York Wed. night, the 20th. I will see you immediately after you speak Thursday afternoon—I must present our Institute's research sub-proposals to the GEOSECS principal investigators Fri. morning. Unfortunately must come home Sunday, maybe even Saturday night, (I must be here at the Institute for the Monday budget meeting)—I hate flying east. Find us a good place in Rhode Island. I will be very happy to meet you.

Love,

Raoul

On Tuesday, September 19, Raoul is awakened by a V-2 air attack over the Arc de Triomphe. He flails his arms desperately to stop the sputtering weapon, which becomes the alarm clock and wakes up in an explosion of gas and dust and flames to find himself undamaged in his miniature Place Dauphine flat. The telephone is still ringing.

"Allo?" Still half asleep.

"Allo, Gautier. It's me. I'm sorry to awaken you but the news is not good. They took him to the hospital this morning in an ambulance. No prognosis yet." Jules Farley was talking about Guy Leysson.

"My God, he hasn't finished the budget planning and the budget meeting is this coming Monday!"

"That's why I'm calling. We must meet tomorrow and we must finish it—the budget must be typed, circulated, and go out to Paris to arrive by next Tuesday. Our national meeting is Thursday! Leysson plays his cards very close to the chest. For us to pick up the pieces in time will be exceedingly difficult. I just called the hospital: Leysson's there. Raoul, you'll have to make the final presentation here next Monday; for this to happen we need to meet about this at 9:30 tomorrow morning, my office."

"Fine."

"See you then."

"Wait, wait! Jules! Tomorrow? Tomorrow I leave in the morning for Paris, at 10. My plane to New York is at 13:30. We must meet on the budget *tonight. Today. Right now.*"

"Not possible. We need Girard Beaumont and he won't be back until late tonight. He must attend—if not we will suffer his paranoia—he will accuse us of stealing his research money and his subdirectorship. Tomorrow at 9:30, my office."

Gautier hangs up. He pictures all exigencies. He never goes to Rhode Island. He goes to Rhode Island, arrives late. He goes to the Charles de Gaulle airport, but mistaking the flight, he continues on to New Caledonia, never to stop in New York at all.

The rest of Tuesday prolongs the nightmare. Hustling into the laboratory later that morning Raoul finds a note from Jules on his bench: "LEYSSON TAKEN INTO SURGERY. STILL NO PROGNOSIS."

Mlle. Rigaud has five file drawers on the floor of her office, papers everywhere. She has not combed her auburn hair. The '77 budget cannot be located. The '78 budget, last year's financial record for the entire research institute, is scattered and scratched on random pieces of paper, fragments she found hidden in unexpected places, with pages missing. Names and job descriptions appear separated from salaries and personnel pay scales as if to avoid the distasteful correlations. Titles: *Subdirecteur, Charge-de-recherche,*

Maître-de-recherche, Recherchant, Assistante, all like severed fingers hanging on threads. Ligaments so torn that Gautier, Farley, and Beaumont feel more like emergency room surgeons than ad hoc budget committee members. Mlle. Rigaud is triage nurse.

Finally at 7:15 that evening, the appropriate documents are neatly in place on the long table where only yesterday red-inked chromatogram readouts were strewn. Gautier shakes himself to an unwelcome piece of awareness. He will miss René's talk. He will not be in Rhode Island by Thursday afternoon. He rushes to the phone. He dials. He endures long pauses, arcane buzzings and ringings. He hears a deep American-accented voice: he pictures the out-sized youth, the shy Yale gas-chromatographer computer genius. This must be David, her marijuana-smoking methane-measuring colleague from an Iowa farm. "Dr. Pemberlain teaches her class from one to two. She's not here. May I take a message?"

Raoul debates. Should he leave a message they can't be together Thursday night? No. He needs to tell her himself.

"Yes, please tell René she should call Gautier in Gif—in Paris—as soon as she completes her class." She will know I'm still in France, Gautier thinks and then says aloud, "Tell her it's very important."

"Goat . . .?" says the voice.

"Gau-tier, i-e-r."

"Goatier," he responds brightly, "Comparative adjective. Goatier in gay Paree. Got it."

Click. Tuesday night in bed in his tiny telephoneless, toilet-less room in Gif at 11:10 he remembers that René never returned his call. Did she even try? The switchboard, eureka, closes, at 7:30, that's only 1:30 in Connecticut.

The next morning, Wednesday, at 9:40 Gautier looks across the secretary's large desk. He manhandles Mlle. Rigaud's manicure and forces her to look into his eyes. "I'm going into this budget meeting now," he demands, "but I need you to phone Dr. Pemberlain at Yale—you must speak to her personally—no messages. Tell her I will miss our Thursday afternoon meeting because of our budget crisis. Tell her I will definitely be in Rhode Island by Friday morning—perhaps even late Thursday night. Tell her the director is in the hospital. Please tell her to please wait for me."

"Monsieur Gautier, I cannot speak English well enough to say that."

"Dr. Pemberlain speaks French well enough. She will understand if you speak slowly and repeat your message. But Mademoiselle, it is very important to me that she receives my message."

The budget meeting is ridiculous. The business that, had Gautier not had to placate Beaumont, should have been finished in an hour, finally ends in four. Mlle. Rigaud stays until the job is finished: the Gautier January-to-December 1979 budget of the Institute for Atmospheric Chemistry is typed, and Beaumont rejects it. Typed again, it is rejected again. The new, fourth-round budget is extremely clear and trim, far more so than the confused '78 model from which they worked so feverishly.

Even Beaumont accepts it. Gautier, Beaumont, Farley, and two research students celebrate dinner like businessmen. Satiated, contemplative, Raoul returns to his office through the dark and calm outside the laboratory. The secretaries and the scientists have left. A fungal odor pervades from nubile agarics. Outside his wood-paneled window the damp shrubbery glistens in the wavering lights of Gif. The new budget filed safely away for next Monday's presentation, Gautier chooses his slides, acetate overheads, and papers for his American journey. He picks up the small items he needs from the mess on his desk and packs them in his leather case. Then he sees Mlle. Rigaud's note:

I CALLED YALE UNIVERSITY 14:30 (8:30 THERE) AND NO ANSWER. SO I WAITED UNTIL JUST BEFORE I LEFT AT 18:00—IT WAS APPARENTLY NOON THERE AND EVERYONE WAS OUT TO LUNCH. I'M SO SORRY M. GAUTIER BUT DR. PEMBERLAIN STILL DOES NOT HAVE YOUR MESSAGE.

G. RIGAUD

Gautier grabs the phone.

"Hello." Same sonorous male voice.

"Dr. Pemberlain, please."

"She left the lab for the day. She's off to Rhode Island this afternoon. She presents her paper at a meeting there tomorrow afternoon. I think she's staying there tonight."

On Thursday, René delivers her talk to the attentive audience like a concert pianist. J. T. Tolly, Jr., is especially attentive. For prelude, she interprets past data, showing the widely used methods to be invalid. Disparate instruments yielded incomparable results that nevertheless were compared. Even units (weight/time: volume/time) were left unstated so that numbers, inconsistently collected, had ambiguous meanings. She presents a plan of action, a remedy for the incongruous. She projects illustrations of her equipment, bright slides that illuminate her description. She presents proof that, in the pond, all methane she and David measure comes from bacteria, not rocks.

A huge fraction of the sun's power translated into photosynthate (food, wood) goes to form the methane; some 8 percent of the total production of organic carbon per year becomes methane. She finishes by posing several new problems. What is the role of methane in atmospheric processes? Does it stabilize the atmospheric oxygen? Why is so much photosynthetic energy expended to form this highly reactive gas? Enthusiastic applause and harumphs of approval die down into mutters of "I told you so," the highest compliment for a scientific paper. She smiles, a little shyly.

She combs the audience for Gautier. She was anticipating his approbation. He is not here. Charles de Gaulle, Gare du Nord. He's a Tin Man; cool exterior, no heart. Again she is deceived by the evasive Frenchman. However he got it, he deserves the damn scar. Is she not duped again like the rural bumpkin that she underneath still feels herself to be? Her naïve pride sours into humiliation. Does everyone in the room know she's been stood up still another time?

Gautier simultaneously disembarks at Kennedy Airport, half an hour late. Labyrinthine bus and Amtrak schedules move him to the desperate measure of renting a car.

Two hours after disembarking he has rented what appears to be a taxicab. He clumsily follows confusing airport signs in the rain. North. Driving away in the Chevrolet Caprice, he fumbles in the dark to turn off the radio, which had startled him to attention with rock and roll. He explains in his mind to René about Gif, the crisis, Guy Leysson's prostate, the budget, Beaumont's power-tripping paranoia that led him to delay and reject, reject and delay the budget plan.

She must respect his unfailing responsibility to science, to his institute.

He recites, into the ringing silence, a poem to himself. Over and over, following the metronome of the windshield wipers.

> *La mer. La mer*
> *Toujours recomencée*
> *On recompense après une pensée*
> *Qu'un long regard*
> *Sur le calme des dieux*

Again and again he repeats the poem aloud to keep himself from speeding, from falling asleep, from self-recrimination.

New York has become so congested that, exasperated, he takes nearly four hours to circumnavigate the megalopolis. In the end the route he chose to avoid Manhattan at all cost saves him not even ten minutes.

The rain becomes heavier. The freeways at New Rochelle curve north to Providence. He can build into his '79 budget a salary for her. When he returns Monday that will be easy—

far easier than it would have been last year or the years before. She will spend a whole year, paid by the institute. Live with him!

Raoul wonders what it would be like to introduce this scientific girl to his sister Janine? How will Sézanne seem to a rural Canadian atmospheric chemist? Another farm town, really—Champagne grapes and brie farmer cheese instead of prairie. The Sézannaises will close upon her, even his mother. They consider Raoul's family outsiders after so many years anyway. He will take her, hand-in-hand, to his steep, flat-topped boulder. René and he will visit the scene and he will tell her of his experiments. Yes, he'll even tell her the story of his scar.

They will be a team, colleagues, coauthors. An island of work, this is all he ever wanted. They will be castaways, isolated from administration, bosses, *fonctionaires*. He will support her every professional need.

WELCOME TO MASSACHUSETTS! reads the large green-and-white sign.

Massachusetts? Connecticut leads to Rhode Island, and Providence was in Rhode Island, wasn't it? He is jolted out of his reverie and tries to orient himself. Fumbling for the map, he drives to the road's shoulder. His stomach turns over. He had forgotten how easterly everything went on the Atlantic coast. He never should have been north of Hartford. He meant to go east toward Boston when he went north toward Canada, past Hartford.

He arrives at 1:50 a.m. at the Howard Johnson Motel in Providence. Although exhausted, he is buoyed by a frenzy of anticipation, a storm of eagerness. He asks the somnolent clerk for Dr. Pemberlain. She's gone, checked out.

"When did she go?" he asks.

"About 9 p.m. I had the suitcase she left at the desk. But she checked out at noon."

Gautier grabs his room key. He leaves his bags and papers in the yellow car. He pants up to the second-floor room, negotiates the unforgiving telephone instructions.

"Hello?"

"Yes, hallo, René?"

"Yes, Gautier."

"Where are you?"

"Where am I? Home, of course. Aren't *you* calling *me* here—I'm home with my parakeet. Where are you? Or perhaps more germane: where were you?"

"Oh, I have a long story to tell you. But I must return Saturday night. The subdirector is dying of cancer—I must defend the budget on Monday—therefore Saturday I must leave. You must come back and let me explain."

"I must come back? Gautier, I thought I was in love with you, but I'm cured. My fever for you I see now wasn't love— love is mutual. It was a sex-engendered fever, like a venereal disease, inflamed by an unnatural enthusiasm for your work. That much was mutual at least. Anyway, I am cured. Good luck in your life."

Gautier sits heavily with Steve Ramsey, Alton Brainerd, Donald Peterson and two of their students Saturday morning September 23. He drinks watered coffee at Lum's in Providence, McDonalds arch in sight. He is somewhere in America, 1978. He diverts himself from unwelcome talk by focusing on the important: atmospheric gas concentrations, efficient chemical equations of common gas sinks, gradients, and inversion layers. His colleagues discuss current films. *Who'll Stop the Rain, Coming Home* with Jane Fonda and John Voigt, *Madame Rosa, Go Tell the Spartans!* and *The Deer Hunter*, about Southeast Asia and Hollywood. Whatever were they saying now? Gautier sips his cold, pseudocoffee. He realizes that he now understands these Americans, though not their movies or their idle remarks about women. The shop talk is much clearer to him now—and even the social prattle, so much did René expand his spoken English. He finally understands and speaks adequately.

"Isn't Gautier the new director?" asks Donald Peterson of Alton Brainerd without even looking at Gautier.

"Sure, he must be—he's just not saying anything. 'Not a word spake he mehr than what was neede'," quotes Brainerd. Not even Chaucer's English cuts through Raoul's fog.

"What?" he asks.

"Aren't *you* the new director of the Atmospheric Chemistry Institute at Gif?" Ramsey was smiling provocatively.

"No," says Gautier.

"If not yet, you certainly will be soon. Leysson is *hors de combat*. Beaumont's an asshole—not a scientist—he couldn't control a toy car, let alone an experiment. And Farley, who has such a terrible accent, commands this much respect outside the Institute." He pinches his fingers like a hand puppet. "Come on, don't play hard to get, Gautier—you have to remember your old friends, now that you're in big time science. Of course you'll be director. You probably are already."

"I am not playing hard to anything. I am just a researcher."

"Well, are you going to take the job? And if you don't take it, who will? Who will oversee the GEOSECS subcontract? Hell, Gif will lose the contract if you have no leadership," Ramsey continues.

"No one knows yet. Leysson may live—he may be OK. I can't take that job—it will end my research. I will never do anything meaningful again."

"Yeah, but you can't afford not to take it either," pipes up Peterson.

Raoul falls silent. That much he didn't want to think about. What was he to do? Let the institute become a sinecure for science, where no real science happens anymore, just as the materials science division did when Michaud took the job in Los Angeles? Like the biology labs at the Laboratory of Evolution of Organized Beings on Boulevard Raspail when Monsieur André Hollande died and Professor P.-P. Grassé retired? Strong directors set the style, the tone, the mood of their entire institute. Anyone bold enough to resist encroaching mediocrity either leaves the institute, or the country—if he can find funding.

"So, Raoul, will you be director? You have to take the job; you know you do." Ramsey smiles at Brainerd, at Peterson, at the two staring students. And back to Raoul.

"I don't know. Don't ask me now." Raoul fantasizes about the equipment he will buy, the science left to be done in a reorganized institute. He will coordinate the GEOSECS atmospheric subcontract. He will run the joint program with the AINDEX, the electron microprobe-scanning electron microscope facility at Toulouse. He will install a new ion probe at Gif within a year. He will buy a new column for his gas chromatograph and before 1980 refurbish the mass spectrometer now in disarray at the physical chemistry institute. He will discharge Guy Leysson's petty, tyrannical blonde secretary and replace her with Mlle. Rigaud. He'll help her improve her performance, and her English. He will establish a new salary scale for the assistants, the janitorial staff, and the apprentice students. He will begin to merge the libraries of his Atmospheric Chemistry Institute with those of the Agricultural and Biological Chemistry Institutes. He will return to represent his institute at Gif at the 1980 GEOSECS Atmospheric Subcommittee meetings. He will reinstate weekly laboratory meetings. In person, quarterly, he will represent atmospheric chemistry at all sessions of CNRS physical and chemical science committees in Paris, quai Anatole France. Next time he enters the grand foyer at this Parisian center of science administration where significant policy decisions are made, he will be recognized as the symbol for the thriving field of atmospheric trace gas chemistry. Indeed, most closely, most critical to his present mood—if this is a mood and not simply a way of life—he will deliver the new 1979 Institute budget at Monday's meeting. His conviction and clear presentation will lead them to approve it. They will congratulate him. Without fanfare. These gray science bureaucrats will usher him out of the Monday morning meeting, quai Anatole France, with certainty that French science, this branch anyway, is slated to thrive. He knows that he will do it all well because it has to be done even though he hates it. He will hire, hand-pick the finest scientists in France, the best anglophone post-docs, and fire when necessary. He will insist that Georges Standon take over the CNRS Physical Sciences Study Panel and live, not just commute from New York, no, *live* in Paris, near Quai Anatole France, for at least two years. He will act with surgical speed and certainty.

Dear beautiful René, so smart, so much younger, and so ready to help him in this life, will be gone for good. René and he will forever be on opposite sides of the mid-Atlantic ridge. Each will ride their crustal plates, their continents adrift in opposite directions. Yes. Although he loved her at first sight when she presented her thesis work at Wiesbaden and hated himself for his late arrival at Gare du Nord, he only showed his true self to her once at Wiesbaden, once at Place Dauphine, and in one letter written on the last day of September. Indeed, though he adored her infinitely last summer in Providence, but he cannot alter the habits of nearly half a century. René, the only love he ever knew he gave no chance to know him. He cannot look into someone else's soul. He lacks the methodology.

"Come on, Gautier," pleads Brainerd. "Tell us you'll take the head honcho job. We already know they asked you. We know no one else even has a chance. Anyone else will ruin everything. We need you on our side. Don't be coy—tell us that you'll take the job, that you'll save our science."

Don Peterson can't stop grinning. Ramsey, Brainerd, and the two students also smile. This infuriates Gautier. He sees them in his mind's eye violating his private life as they throw open all his files. They strew his papers, even her love letters, across the dirty streets of Providence. No one yet stops smiling, pleasantly.

"Do *answer* us anyway," says Ramsey in a kindly way, sensing Gautier's black mood.

"I don't know," he repeats. "Don't ask me again. Don't ask me now. I just don't know."

But of course he knows.

THE ESTIMATOR
(Georges)

For Nature is a stranger yet
The ones who cite her most
Have not passed her haunted house
Nor simplified her ghost.
To pity those who know her not
Is helped by the regret
That those who know her, know her less
The nearer her they get.

Emily Dickinson, 1830–1886
Last stanza of "What Mystery Pervades a Well"
Nature poem #96

International science—Big Science—is a deal with the devil. How else could a football field-sized space station be hurled into Earth orbit? How else might three people land on the surface of Mars, live there as if it were Arizona, and return to Earth three years later to talk about the windstorms and the dry dust? Big Science tempts only those whose survival depends on the kindness of strange funding agencies, only those scientists with few alternatives.

Georges Standon flips open Cerda's *The Development of Scientific Thought and Method*, his light reading for the trip—not really work. History of science is light fare, fun, he thought. He had not indulged in pleasure reading since he left New York to cross the Atlantic nine hours earlier. Nor had he even touched his mandatory assignment for

tomorrow's session. He begins with the joys of Democritus
in the first chapter, in English translation of course.

> By custom, there is sweet,
> by custom bitter,
> by custom hot,
> by custom cold,
> by custom color—
> but really atom and void
>> Democritus of Abdera (fl. 400 BC)
>> Diehls fragment 135

He tosses the book on the bed, among the menagerie of
papers. His task is to synthesize and translate by tomorrow
morning. He looks down from the window of the Hotel des
Trois Continents at the Renaults, Peugeots, and Saabs. St.
Germain was sweet and melancholy—even if not quite the
same. He had flown overnight and slept crookedly in his only
good suit. More tired than hungry, he tries to classify his
fuzzy feeling: *degouté, ecoeuré, dégoûtant;* no, not disgusting,
just muddled. Distasteful. Tomorrow morning, 9 o'clock
will be 9 o'clock even if it is still only 3 a.m. for him.

The European Space Agency Shuttle report is early on the
agenda, and he will have to present it whether or not Bob
Fleigel makes it in on time from Cal Tech. Fleigel knows more
about the complexities than Georges—launch windows,
landing readiness—but after seventeen years with ESA panels,
he still can't even respond to a polite *"bonjour."* Georges's
fluent French will influence the panel far more than Fleigel's
shuttle politics. Six of nine ESA representatives will be French.

Two Germans and a Dutchman, all fluent in English, also speak French better than Fleigel speaks English.

Georges sits on the bed and leans back on NASA Shuttle handouts, graphs of a shuttle-launchable communications satellite design, a Voyager photograph of Jupiter marked by two moons. That was pile one. An artist's rendering portrayed the Shuttle upright against its launch gantry, bloated with the huge hydrogen-oxygen tanks he thought too dangerous to be used—he wouldn't have to talk about that.

The shuttle payload bay and its construction, the casing into which—if approved—the Europeans will place their Spacelab, are in pile two with details of the orbiting transportation system. On the crowded plane Georges, with great difficulty, sorted the grant proposals, first by country of senior principal investigator (England, France, Netherlands, USA, West Germany), then by subject (particles and fields, gravity, ionospheric physics, life sciences, materials processing), then alphabetically by name and institution: Brainerd, A., Gautier, R., Peterson, D., Ramsey, S., Massachusetts Institute of Technology: Stratospheric ozone. Haas, R. S., Van Warden, C., University of Colorado: Global climate models. MacNeil, C. F., University of Pennsylvania: Gravimetric sensors above the meristem in plant-root-tips.

The Spacelab must bring perfectly planned experiments into orbit—give the shuttle a raison d'être. Are the Germans and Dutch going to contribute a greater proportion of the space lab costs, the French less? Georges recalls a French astronomer who called the space lab "expensive pseudoscience."

Fleigel and cohort want the science done and the bills paid on time. Dutch, German, French, whichever government pays is all the same to them. How can Georges fashion this suitcase full of information into thirty minutes that will ensure French participation? Will anyone there have the authority to commit French funds? Will the French scientists appreciate or resent his New Jersey accent?

Georges absently watches a couple below on the rue de Bourbon le Chateau as they exclude the rest of the world and jaywalk across the street, leaving a bar door swinging behind them. A woman in high-heeled boots tugs at her dachshund's leash, shaking her narrow hips, showing off the smooth straight line of her deeply split red skirt, legs alternately emerging and hiding.

The Left Bank originated as one of those poor neighborhoods across the river from the real city, like Rome's Trastevere. The working poor, bred in squalor, multiplied helpless and hopeless into the present. For more than a century it had become alive with music and motion at a low price, a bohemian paradise. By the time he and Odile moved to rue d'Anglais it had become chic but still affordable. Now Hermès stores and million-dollar penthouse condos sported the summer alpine and winter Riviera set. Money flowed in, displacing the bohemians. It was reminiscent of the trend on Bleecker Street in Greenwich Village.

In his native habitat, the Earth and Space Science Department at City College, Georges Standon's scientific contributions are prodigious. His work on the lunar samples returned from the Apollo missions, on Martian volcanic activity, and on meteorite crater bombardment alone fill two bound volumes.

He lies down on the Second Empire bed, gazes at the

chandelier. Rolling over and sitting up, he looks at himself in the long mirror on the armoire. I still look much younger, well at least a little younger, than my advanced age, he says aloud, sliding his hand into his pajama trousers. A bell tolls, from a church he thinks; the tolling continues, steadily, rhythmically, far past any count of twelve. Ringing *nones* maybe, or *compline,* some un-American canonical hour for monks to gather in prayer. He thinks of *"Frère Jacques"*— only for Catholic countries—the children's song about monks rising for prayer:

Are you sleeping, are you sleeping,
Brother Jacques, brother Jacques?
Drop your cock and ring the clock,
drop your cock and ring the clock,
Ding-dang-dong! Ding-dang-dong!

Georges moves the skin back and forth to the rhythm of the church bell. No one else to please, no demands, no boredom, and certainly never any tears. If he had remained a *celibataire*— a *masturbataire?*—what happened yesterday never would have happened, and tomorrow morning's shuttle report by now would be ready.

The smell of St. Germaine de Près, the quaint *oo-bah-oo-bah* of French sirens, coalesces with the relief and ennui of climax to jolt forward his memory of Odile, of the St. Germain apartment. He was twenty-five—how now has he come to be fifty-eight? He read in the airline magazine between the ads that new research claims that women's interest in sex diminishes by thirty-five, and their interest in love by forty. Men's interest in love fades earlier, and even sex is no longer supposed to be compelling to men after fifty-five. Why was it still such a drain on his attention? He *must* concentrate on the maximum French commitment to the Spacelab payload —with proper science of course —into the NASA Shuttle?

Georges, for a living, calculates chances. What are the chances of low-probability but high-consequence events such as meteoric impacts, asteroid collisions? What are the probabilities of the existence of extrasolar planets and their moons? He is a professional, a human calculator of strangely improbable events. What are the chances that medium-dense interstellar clouds encounter the sun? And if the interstellar clouds are really dense, how does the probability of encounter increase? Not statistically significant. After all, what does Georges do if not calculate probabilities of low-frequency events, such as getting laid regularly at age fifty-eight?

Rare events of planetary collision, like the 25,000-year-old boloid that formed the great Barringer meteorite crater at Winslow, Arizona, are his forté. The impact of a planetary-scale object hitting Earth with enough energy to rip off deep layers of the Earth's crust—the Tapeats Sandstone, the Bright Angel Shale, the Muav Limestone, the Redwall Limestone, the Supai Formation, and the Hermit Shale. They flipped the crust like pancakes, leaving the geologically oldest layers on top, the freshest layers of sediment beneath, face down on the griddle. He has devoted his life to such descriptions, to the publication of probabilities.

So what in hell was the probability that yesterday all three of the women of his life—one of them presumed dead—would appear simultaneously? Fewer than one in a million? How many days in his life? 21,372. How many people in New York? More than seven million—but empirical evidence has always shown him that the probability of encountering someone you know in the city, on a given day—especially someone you prefer to avoid—is roughly 1:1, sometimes 2:1.

Yesterday's shock-formed crater impresses itself on his emotional landscape, penetrating the compartments of his triune brain, leaving scattered debris in the corners of his bilingual soul.

Odile gave birth to Alain in 1956, just after their third anniversary. He met her in late 1952. Why had his research supervisor at rue de la Université, Arrondisement 6, sent him to the library rue de l'École de Medicine? Georges had been working in the physics lab for two months since arriving in France. Although his French was still poor, he made himself understood. The medical library was huge, the ceilings extended far above the mezzanine where ancient books were stored on shelves from floor to ceiling, tall ladders used to reach them. Rows of beautiful oak tables lined the main reading hall. He submitted his library slip at *vitrine deux*. Georges retains perfect images of each of his subsequent movements. After what seemed to be a tiresome wait, a somber old woman gave him the immense, cumbersome book, bound in beige. He took the tome back to the long reading desk to look up whatever it was he had been sent to find.

In that ancient library on that overcast day, the only light diffused from dim, distant chandeliers thirty feet above, the *plafond* decorated with tarnished rococo frippery. The other readers at the long oak tables had small modern reading lamps, clean white light emanating from a panel in front of each of their seats, but Georges could not find his light switch. Carefully he put the question: "Ou se trouve la lumière?" to the girl sitting next to him. She looked up from her huge anatomy text. "C'ést facile," she answered and pointed to a panel of light switches behind the footrests. Somehow his desk light refused to turn on. She switched it on for him with an amused, teasing smile. He smiled back wryly. He explained that he wasn't familiar with the medical library, that he did physics; they whispered to keep the other readers from hearing them, an intimate complicity. She was serious, enthusiastic, and bright.

A month later they rented a tiny apartment on the sixth floor near St. Severin on rue d'Anglais. She studied neuroanatomy all day, and he came home from the lab to her comfort. He began to feel at home in France, and in French, in the best way—the classical way. He fell deeply in love with Odile, a Frenchwoman, and nearly a scientist.

Georges pauses in his reminiscences. What had changed? This room at the Trois Continents Hotel must be the same now as it was then . . . the decor certainly dates from before 1952. Their old apartment on rue d'Anglais is probably still there too. He could walk by the next day to see; it wasn't far.

The first years of marriage were painful. Impossible for him. How were they for her? She studied furiously, the best student in her medical school class. She needed him home for dinner at a fixed time—any fixed time planned in advance, so she could return to evening lectures or to the library. But even then, or perhaps especially then, he balked at rules. He won't be told when to come, when to go, what to do. He grabbed for her with lust and love twice a day, three times even. *Non,* she would say, *non!* I have an exam tomorrow. Wide awake at dawn, she would roll over to him with hope, kisses, anticipation. Love, not sex, she whispers. No, this is the day of his planning session for the big calculations. No, this is the morning of the weekly lab meeting and he is already late.

She cooked indifferently, but there was always food on the table. She struggled with the laundry, hung faded underwear outside on an old cord between rainstorms. Odile shopped, cleaned. Eyes coursing the armoire, chandeliers, *plafond,* Georges realizes he did not appreciate that while she studied medicine she also did everything else—for him—the housework, the shopping, the bills.

Marriage, and even the memory of marriage, torments Georges. Tonight that long-ago exasperation returns. Often he failed to call her—to return from the lab on time for dinner. He did not call, dammit. He recalls with guilt the old pleasant sense of revenge. So what? He was too busy to call her. She shed tears, voiced recriminations. They bickered, verbally scratching through hundreds of prolonged, too-late discussions.

After three years in Paris, Georges accepted the job offer from City College. Odile followed him to New York, her medical program aborted, no degree. After six months of reference librarians, phone inquiries, professional school catalogues, admissions discussions, and guidance counselor courtesy, Odile found a neuroanatomy program that accepted her funny French training. The redundancy of the New York courses vexed her. She spoke rarely and tensely of cold trains and long commutes. She hated New York City: too cold, too hot, too crowded, and too ugly. Their apartment was too tawdry, too noisy; their furnishings too dirty, too flimsy.

Georges stood over the porcelain kitchen sink one evening watching bits of carrots and radishes swirl down. He imagined seeing the effect of the Coriolis force on vegetables and lamented forgetting the hydrodynamic equation, when the telephone rang. "Answer it!" she cried out from behind the closed bathroom door. "If it's for me, tell them I'm pregnant." Georges did not hang up on the wrong number for a full three minutes. The phone cord dangled on her words. It was March of their first year back in the States. She vomited through her final exams. Yet, even in the American tongue that she complained would always be foreign to her, she finished first in her class. This achievement filled her with even greater anxiety.

Georges knew she wasn't happy about the pregnancy: she was trapped in domestic servitude in New York. He was the cage-keeper. Now she was hand- and foot-cuffed, immobile, chained to her fetus by the umbilicus. Georges regarded birth control and baby-making as women's problems. Because his name ends in "s" everyone assumes Georges is French-Canadian, but he isn't. His mother's family is Italian Catholic. His father's family is Irish-Catholic as far as he knows. No one in his immediate family even practiced Catholicism anymore, nor birth control either. He never reckoned that his brilliant female anatomist would ignore the exigencies of her own body. If she did not want the pregnancy, Georges assumed, she would control potential birth.

The marriage, already too late to fix, was terminated by the birth. Odile was delivered of Alain in a crowded, hurried, unfriendly Manhattan hospital that December, from which she insisted on escaping as soon as she could. At home, Georges's solicitousness was half-hearted, his rare help more frustrating than useful. Odile recovered from birth as she took care of all three—the infant, the husband, her sleep-deprived self. The colicky frantic baby cried all night; Odile struggled to find child care and to study. She quietly burned in stoical tension. Academically, these were Georges's most productive years.

In the dim light of the bedside reading lamp Georges stares unseeing at pamphlets, letters, viewgraphs, and glossies. Rubbing his bare feet on the tops of piles one and three, Georges wonders if his productivity is a precise function of family neglect. How—in what units—should he measure neglect of his infant son?

Odile became a first-class diagnostician of nervous disorders. In spite of the discord between his frenetic parents, Alain was a joyous child—his outgoing gaiety filled the silence of the cramped apartment.

Odile traveled extensively and so did Georges. They delayed the inevitability of the break. During the planning for Apollo missions he whizzed—by plane of course—incessantly between Houston and Pasadena. Georges's watch stayed set three hours behind New York, so frequently did he have to travel to California. Tonight, Georges feels the slip of both of the tall paper piles, lets his mind slide completely off the Spacelab. Odile attended a neurophysiology symposium in Argentina. She never returned.

The puzzle pieces of Georges's life—his curriculum vitae—do not fit. Three years are missing; his publication list is blank from 1960 to 1963. No output. He authored not a single paper during an entire three years. Yet he taught. He was employed. He was healthy. The three-year lapse seems incomprehensible to the university's tenure and promotion committee.

His memory of Argentina is a tunnel, a whirling four-colored map. Three times in three years he left Alain with his own mother to seek Odile. On the '62 trip he lectured to the Argentinian Association for Astronomy. His prediction that glassy vesiculated particles would be found on the lunar regolith somehow left him empty. He found no joy in its verity. The abstract of the work he presented in '63 in Argentina was a gem of clarity and insight. Published in 1965 as a full paper, it brought to him the Faculty Publication Merit Award of City College.

The trips to Argentina exacerbated his excruciating guilt: he lacked compulsion to work. Even the three-week abandonment of his son hurt him deeply. He should have taken Alain to the Argentine. Georges now, tonight, still cannot answer the question: what if I had found her? Days of searching, scraps of information, dead-end clues. For years the unresolved worry, questions about Odile's fate, his own ambiguity, left him feeling like a man unfinished. He never takes refuge in happy memories of life before she disappeared. He is goaded by his anger, the guilty feeling that Alain was orphaned.

Georges left Alain more and more with his own mother in New Jersey. His last investigation trip was less frenzied: a two-week lecture tour in Argentina, the first week in Buenos Aires. His official visit to the forty-inch reflector telescope the second week at Los Altos de la Montaña opened many doors; to plush and rustic offices, to luxurious and sparse homes. A few months after the last trip, late in '64, he received by mail two contradictory Argentine legal notices. The predictable Latin bureaucratic paradox. One was her death certificate, the second was his marriage annulment. He deciphered the Spanish through French cognates. His paperback dictionary, Spanish-to-French, was totally inadequate to the task. The fine-print formalism on the two documents was maddening and he trusted no one, man or woman, well enough to share the pain of Argentine bureaucracy. He filed them away unexplained. Slowly in their cardbox coffin they turned yellow, joining the yellow baby pictures, Alain's birth certificate, the original Paris marriage license. They fade with other fading memories.

Odile had appeared at a La Plata neurophysiology meeting in 1960, Georges learned. She had spoken at a Buenos Aires symposium two months later. She had submitted on time her single-authored paper on dopamine and serotonin for the symposium publication. Georges received a photocopy of the half-page of the newsletter of the Buenos Aires Sociedad de Neurofisiologia from the wife of an astronomer. He knew nothing more. He still knows nothing more. His wife was swallowed by a country.

Alain was taken by Georges's mother. Grandma Barbara is good with children. She inclined to spoil Alain out of pity, the poor boy who'd lost his mother so young. Georges tried to leave the Argentine years behind by immersion in his work. He guiltily enjoyed his new freedom. He found, too easily, many casual sleeping companions. He arose early, shaved, showered, and left for work by 7:15 a.m., as usual. Whatever her name, her occupation, her job, Georges bought her coffee to encourage her to leave the apartment at 7:15 with him. Month-long intervals of matelessness. Wanton, autoinduced, or absence of any activity, and actions that lack any complication were not only inevitable, he'd welcomed them.

Alain and he played together nearly every Sunday: football, baseball, basketball, as either spectators or participants. One week they climbed the Presidential Range in New Hampshire. They started with the ascent of Mt. Washington—a memorable foggy walk took them to the hut of the Lake of the Clouds. Trekking behind, watching Alain's strong sure legs that day, Georges felt old for the first time. Father and son assembled hi-fi equipment, built two stereo receivers. In his early teens, Alain worked with Georges every Sunday for months to put together a Questar telescope. Together they observed the moons of Jupiter: Io, Iapatus, Europa. They photographed the rings of Saturn and its moon Titan.

Georges remembers clearly one Sunday unlike the others, early April sunshine cut by a chill breeze in their panting and shouting lungs. From the hilltop behind a vacant lot near Grandma Standon's house, the panorama was sliced vertically by TV towers, smokestacks, chimneys, squat oil storage tanks. Out of the grass surrounding the baseball diamond peeked nubile crocus buds. Georges was happy with the physical weariness of sport. Alain was quick, nimble-limbed, clear-breathed; more than anything, thought Georges, he's young. Georges heaved the ball like a shotput. "OK, here it comes, Dad," shouted Alain, the baseball's effortless arc like a comet dragging Alain's arm behind it. The ball traced its trajectory in Georges's mind, the history of a flight and fate made rational. Dx/dt declining as the ball went up, zeroing for an infinitesimal instant at the summit, then changing sign, the ball descending, the first derivative of the function negative. The ball plopped, rolled out of reach.

Georges bent gamely at the waist to dig the baseball out of hiding in a crocus clump. He felt a stab; something momentous occurred in his lower back. In an epiphany, he became conscious, for the first time in his life, that he *had* a lower back.

"Come on, Dad, you got it?" he heard Alain call.

"Just a second, something's happened," yelled Georges, dragging himself like a hunchback toward a green park bench, ball still gripped in his glove.

He wilted onto the bench, lay supine along the seat, legs bent off the end, glove hand in his lap. Winded, he looked into the air at the changing light. The New Jersey sky grayed ominously. Alain looked at him quizzically, then sat down heavily beside him on the bench. "What's wrong, Dad?" he asked. As he saw that Georges was in pain, he said worriedly, "Sorry—sorry I bumped down so hard—what's up?"

Still too out of breath and awash in pain to make an excuse, Georges grunted. Then he caught his son's serious brown-eyed gaze. Smiling gently, he drew in his breath, and let him in. "I picked up the ball the wrong way; I guess I strained my back."

Alain looked at him anxiously. He spoke abruptly—a seeming non sequitur. "Dad . . . am I French?" he asked.

"French? Why do you ask? Well, your mother was French; I suppose that makes you half-French. I'm not a bit French, though, you know. Why?"

"So where's she from?"

"She was born in Paris. Why do you ask?"

"Why did she leave us?"

"What do you mean, leave us? She went to Argentina and she died in an accident."

"But, what bothers me . . ." Alain hesitated, eager to reach out, trying to keep something flowing through the tenuous filament that connects his father to himself. "What gets me is why she left to go to Argentina to begin with. It's a long way."

Alain's gaze was pushed downward by his lowering brow. Georges had always avoided thinking this way, even on his detective trips. He now, on a gray New Jersey hillside, was flooded with an absolute loneliness.

"Why did she go?" Georges repeated the question, slowly, and again. He saw his incapacity, not for love, but for sharing of himself. He could not share. Love was what he had felt for her, what he felt for Alain now. He did not know what to say, or how to say it. He cleared his throat, ran a hand over his face and through his hair. He retreated into rationality.

"She must have wanted to go to Argentina more than she wanted to stay and take care of us," Alain said.

"No," Georges answered. "She didn't want to leave us. She was very pleased to have been invited to speak in Argentina about her work. They sent her an airplane ticket. They arranged her speaking engagement. I was proud of her. She didn't want to leave us; it was a sad and freakish accident that she never came back."

"I don't know. I don't feel French," Alain said. "I really don't like being half-French either. I've been sort of working up to telling you this. I talked to Grandma about it—she said I should tell you. But, well—like my name. Would you mind if I spelled it without the 'i'—'Alan,' like I say it—from now on? Would you feel bad if I dropped the 'i'? I hope you're not mad. . . ."

"No, of course I'm not mad. I don't mind at all. Tell you what: I'll drop the 's' from the end of my name too, if you like." His son squinted up quickly to see his grin, met his eyes for the first time in a few minutes. Alain smiled dubiously in acknowledgment, as if his lips were under the control of one puppeteer and his brows another, then dropped his eyes. "A lot of people called me George anyway; and most of the rest end up trying to pronounce my last name '*Stan-do*' instead of 'Stand'n,' as if it were French."

They were silent a few moments. "I'm sorry about it, about your mother," Georges tried to explain.

"What was she like?"

"Odile?"

"I don't really remember her."

"Your mother was beautiful and brilliant, strong-willed, quiet. I loved her—I suppose I still do. She was less cheerful than you are, less open—very French, really. She worked very hard. We both worked all the time. . . ." Georges trailed off.

"Well, I don't love her; I don't even know her," said his son.

"You didn't really get the chance to know each other. It's too late, now."

"Well, she shouldn't have left, then." He took the ball from Georges's glove, tossed it lightly, then held it up to examine like an apple. The lowering sun shone unveiled by clouds. Horizontal light, warmed by filtering through smog, slanted across the brim of Alain's cap and ruddied the lower half of his face.

"Come on, buddy, let's play. And then let's go back to Grandma's—Christ, I'm hungry all of a sudden." Aware the pain has subsided, but not entirely, he jabs Alain lightly on the shoulder. Georges is pleased when his feeble gesture of affection is accepted by his son naturally, casually. They toss the ball about a bit then return in step, close but not touching, to Grandma Barbara's house.

After the '60–'63 hiatus Georges began to publish again—better journals, more notice, steadily and more frequently. Although his scientific work could be criticized for its lack of design or overall plan, he did attack several major geophysical problems. The impact crater and volcano work were applied to the Apollo lunar research program by several colleagues soon after the publications appeared.

NASA's Planets and Asteroids Working Group, PAAWG, enlisted him to membership in 1965. Science for Georges purged boredom. Far more than a way to earn a living, it was an exciting privilege. Georges valued his own opinions but always attended those of others. He never confused the acceptance of his scientific results with the acceptance of himself. His diligence and confidence in his work, as well as his impartial devotion to science rather than to his own observations and theories, were atypical. Less arrogant than his fellow committee members, Georges never annoyed his committeemen with problems of schedule or of ego. When the department chairman found that Georges not only wrote clearly but also met deadlines, he asked Georges to succeed him. Georges chaired three committees nearly simultaneously from 1967 until 1969. He added the duties of two Apollo committee memberships in late 1968, Lunar Surface Evolution and Johnson Spacecraft Center Steering Board. Word traveled quickly through the NASA decision-making process, first in the provinces—Texas (Houston), California (Moffett Field), W. Virginia (Greenbank) and Virginia (Hampden) —then to the capital. Nominating committees noticed: Georges seems to have no pressing family commitments. He is very good. Honest. Comparisons were made: Van Warden's wife is dying of cancer. Barnfield is slow; he never writes up his or anyone else's ideas. Fleigel has a committed family life. Georges is unencumbered.

For Georges, with the demands on his time and rigid schedules, it became like marriage; or worse, like polygamy, with so many committee assignments, speaking engagements, and rigid class schedules.

For ten years, Georges's life centered more on his work, simplifying; then for the next ten his work became more involved, more complex. His datebook for work also listed the names and telephone numbers of many women, mostly science acquaintances whom he called once or twice but never after the second or third encounter. Only two or three entries, phone numbers and fax numbers, are well-used; others crossed out or sporadically updated. He thinks of Maria Elena with comfort for a moment, her warmth and their affair so long, so uncomplicated and so occasional. But after what happened in New York yesterday, he suspects that he has lost her too. He relished her foreign allure, played up the cosmopolitan chic of his bilingual name.

He was born during the time his parents had discovered *culture*. They were in rebellion against New Jersey–New York suburbia, Pine Barren white trash, New Jersey Italian, and New Jersey ugliness. They played Brandenburg concertos and Poulenc suites while he nursed. They read Proust aloud at night. His mother meant well.

If she hadn't named him Georges—'s' *muet* as French colleagues noted to each other of their American colleague—then at the 1975 Paris meetings Madame LeClerc might not have approached him, pointing to his name plate at the round table and saying, "Ah, *Georges*, je suis Denise LeClerc." Considering her assertiveness, though, maybe that was just a pretext. Georges knew her name from the scientific literature. She was perhaps the only woman in the world who had done significant work on the depth of the Martian regolith, the dusty, rubbly cover on Mars. Vivacious and intelligent, she was a first-rate astronomer from the astronomy department of the Université de Liège. From their very first exchange of words the two were animated. Georges was a member of one and a chairman of a second committee to which she also belonged. Furthermore, she and Georges were slated to become members of still another advisory body: a new international group concerned with providing advice to the forthcoming Shuttle principal investigators. Both would oversee the scientific quality of the payloads on the first four Shuttle flights, a three-year commitment at least. They taught precisely comparable courses, she at Liège and he at City College, to the equivalent of seniors and first-year graduate students. They talked seriously, unselfconsciously, and engagingly.

After the final banquet dinner of the '75 meeting in December, they traveled together on the night train from Paris to Liège, where Georges was invited to present a lecture. Something nameless but definite began as the train pulled out of the Charles Roi-Sud station. He could see her again. Perhaps it was the wine, or whispered French evoking images of young Odile and passion on the sixth floor of a St. Severin apartment. Mme LeClerc's warmth and long black hair enticed him. At Compeigne they were gently touching fingers, by Meiberge their hands were clasped, and by Huy Nord they both knew how it would end. At Namur they exchanged home telephone numbers and dates of subsequent joint meetings. When they parted at the Liège station her face was flushed; she glowed as if with early pregnancy. Her smile provoked and her "au revoir" began a new story in his imagination. In the real story, she went off to meet her husband.

But now it is 1976. Georges arrives early at the March '76 Paris ESA-NASA meeting and buries his nose in his papers and frantically tries to arrange his presentation. As often occurs, he is first on the agenda. He glances up after a few minutes to see how much time he has left to whip the talk into shape. The gnomish transparent clock, lacking numerals, has both black hands where one might have hoped to find a nine. Studying it, he realizes it is nearly 9 o'clock.

His presentation begins at 9:50. That the U-shaped table is filling up with privileged joint ESA-NASA delegates, a shuffling to promptly take their seats behind the name signs, is lost on Georges. He sees no shadow across the narrow table right in front of him, nor the LeClerc sign two seats over.

"Bon jour," is all Denise says. He is distracted with the absolute rule to cut his talk to ten minutes. Her glowing eyes shock him. She must have been plotting this encounter for months. What has she in mind? When? For tonight? Noisy Paris, rainy April, tired Georges—not much time. Good.

Georges as a rule never permits indulgences with married women. But experienced women he finds to be far finer in bed than the tentative young ones. Although he rejects the good-bad dichotomy, he recognizes its physiology and likes sin as much as any recovering Catholic. Yet he attends to the commandment to not covet your neighbor's—or anyone else's—wife. That rule is derived, not from God, but from the judgment of very wise men. Denise LeClerc should be no exception.

These ideas do not remain with him long. Mme. LeClerc is delightful, and even enthralling, especially in bed. Her passion, if anything, is intimidating. She is loving, open, and terribly smart. The are separated by four thousand miles, six time zones, semi-annual intervals, her scientist husband, and three adolescent children. Probably she is a little bored with her connubial bliss after twenty years—God knows, sex easily drops out of marriage. Love (sex) may return but lovers (married couples) never do, he muses. The French permit extracurricular activity, he knows. He is just her mistress, that's all.

Georges does not anticipate that this brilliant, lovely woman would fall in love with him. Maybe it is not love. At her age of forty-five how can it be?

Georges returns to New York, to his journal-strewn desk at the university, surrounded by blackboard and paper calculations, harried by student appointments and persistent telephone rings. Back to Maria Elena, grateful that France and Belgium are very far away across the Atlantic.

Tall Marie Elena is open and free. A stewardess for Aeromexico, she flies back and forth between New York and Mexico City three times a week. They have been friends and lovers for three years. The arrangement is fine for both of them. She comes to him on Sundays. If she has conflicts of schedule, she calls on Saturday night. Maria Elena is reliable, affectionate, and undemanding. Although he never asks, she often tidies up his apartment. She always makes his bed after leaving it. She approaches strangers as if they were old friends. She tries out any new language she confronts. Vivacious, she draws him immediately into conversation as if they had just been chatting. She pays rapt attention to him when he talks. She laughs easily. This is the real attraction; she loves to laugh. Maria Elena relishes beautiful clothes, good food, and fine music. Maria Elena never reads anything. She speaks nearly perfect English, but she does not seem particularly literate in any language. Georges does not need to know her intellectual credentials. Their relationship that develops slowly started with immediate physical intercourse. It continues to accumulate: casual intimacy, comforting familiarity, habit. Only later does any other communication flow between them—laughter, giggling. With Maria Elena, he realizes a strange truth: he has never had another friend.

Georges needs all three years of evasive answers to his frank attempts to reconstruct her childhood in Mexico. Maria Elena's father abandoned his cornfield-tomato patch, his wife, and a full dozen children when she, the eldest, was sixteen. A village girl, Georges learned one whispering night when he was too tired to make love, she left the central plateau, the Tepoztecan peak of childhood for the smog and sprawl of the capital when she was seventeen. Her village, forty kilometers from Cuernavaca, was near enough to the capital and major *turista* routes to be indicated as a sight worth seeing on the handouts at downtown hotels. On weekends many cars bumped over the pitted road connecting the village to the outside world. Elena's first contact with Americans then was the same as now: as villager, as waitress, and as stewardess. She knows how to minister to the needs of tourists.

Maria Elena's beauty found her employment in an expensive French restaurant near the embassies. Her youngest sibling was born to her forty-two-year-old mother just prior to her father's final departure. Maria Elena's mother was glad to see the father gone—it was the only sure method of birth control. Maria Elena's younger sister Paquita, six months after she arrived in New York, had herself sterilized. Maria Elena used pills. She knew she didn't want half-a-dozen children, but maybe just one or two sometime.

Over the last three years, Georges's coterie of casual girlfriends had dwindled. His part-time harem was reduced to two women when last winter one of his regulars, a Xerox executive secretary, moved to Atlanta, and a juicy blonde lawyer decided to marry her judge lover after the death of his infirm wife. With two space science committee assignments, two new Ph.D. advisees, and interminable negotiations with his colleagues about the design of the new physical science building, Georges became functionally monogamous in the last year. Only Maria Elena remained. He had given her a key to his Village apartment, for convenience—and she, helpful soul, never seemed to distract him.

Mme. LeClerc called when? Thursday? Yesterday was Friday—no, it was Saturday in New York when he left and it is Sunday night—well, Monday morning—now. For Georges there was no Saturday night, and at this rate there will be no Sunday night either. She phones from her downtown hotel on Thursday evening just as her letter said she would.

Professeur Denise LeClerc wants to know, she said loudly and abruptly as if she were calling trans-Atlantically from her lab, if Georges will let her stay in his apartment Friday night? Would he mind? A well-located room in Manhattan costs at least seventy-five dollars a night; translated from francs that is horribly exorbitant, *n'est-ce pas?* She will stay only Friday night. Early Saturday morning she must leave for Batelle— both locations. She'll fly from LaGuardia to Columbus, Ohio, and then on to Seattle. Sure she may, says Georges, but unfortunately he will not be there. He must be in New Jersey, his son Alan is in from California for a week. Georges has promised dinner with him at Grandma Barbara's before he leaves for France. "Denise," he says hurriedly, "I'll be leaving immediately—as soon as I change my clothes and pick up a few things. Yes," he tells her, "I'll be here at the apartment just long enough to let you in Friday evening. About 5:30."

At 5:50 on Friday, raincoat on, Georges is just about to duck out the door. The doorbell startles him.

She is flushed as she attempts to fall into his arms, which, however, he holds tensely at his side, keys jingling in one hand. "Hi," he offers. She tries to kiss him on the lips, now drawn almost invisibly thin. "No, I have to—here." He struggles to put his keys into her hand, which pursues his evasive fly. *"Je t'aime,"* she says, looking dreamily *engagé*. He had not expected her to arrive 20 minutes late and to immediately warm her hands on his buttocks. Georges pivots away, realizes that way leads into the room, and turns back to the door. She blocks the doorway with her rear end. She triumphantly moves her hands slowly around to the front of his slacks. He takes advantage of the pause to perform mental calculations. He is due at his mother's for dinner at 7:30. It is 6 now. It will take forty minutes from the city to New Jersey, if no traffic—doubtful on Friday night. If traffic, he can hardly be faulted for lateness. Her hands are where it feels very good now. He tells her he is truly sorry he is so pressed. Her hands in his trousers, she uses her thighs to steer him back, with little steps, toward his bed. Mainly body warmth and nips at his open collar warm him. She whispers, "I wait for months for this moment." Her accent washes away anxiety about Alan, the damn traffic, his mother. He begins to pant, and smiles. Flattered, his smiles continues as he reddens and she rolls him into his own bed. Months of tension ease as Georges indulges. The urgency of youth, the frantic personal need so conspicuous to his self-image of thiry years go—disintegrate, disappear. Ironically, even with the urgency of his schedule, in her arms he feels the luxury of time. Now in control of the act, he is capable of indulging her. He avoids a glance at the huge clock just above the bed. But his watch (neither of them removed theirs) tells him how late it is—6:27. He dresses, ties his shoes, grabs his bag. He never even removes one of his socks and this he estimates saves him nineteen seconds, exactly the time equivalent to fish out its mate from the tangled sheets.

"Denise, *chèrie,* please turn out the light and lock the door when you leave here."

"Bien sur," she purrs, ties his scarf loosely, cravat-style, around his neck.

"Yes," he answers, "perhaps we can meet in France or even in Liège next week." Georges still smiles. "Denise, I'm really sorry to go but I leave for France tomorrow night. I'm up to my ears in preparation. *Je suis desolé,* truly, that we haven't more time. It was wonderful to see you again. *Au revoir."*

To him, ruddy faced and warm-limbed, the chill street breeze smells sweet. He walks to his rented parking space in the basement of a high-rise around the corner. He drives absent-mindedly to New Jersey in a surprising paucity of Friday-night out-going traffic. He is only fifteen minutes late for dinner, a delay welcomed by his octogenarian mother. He listens proudly while Alan talks unself-consciously about himself—Silicon Valley shop talk, the young man's musical diversions. Georges enjoys the sweet comfort of family. He sleeps nine hours straight in his old narrow bed, his room retained as in childhood, but tidier.

Georges returns to the city the next afternoon. How can he most efficiently bring back the car to its space and pick up his suitcase? The wind still whips, blustery and painful. Georges estimates as usual: enough time to buy blades, shaving cream, shampoo, and maybe even new boots. Then get home to frantically pack. Exactly enough time to be at Kennedy by 7, park, check in, check his bag. The plane leaves at 8:30. He glances at his watch. Five after four. The good drugstore, just outside the Parker Hotel, around the corner, will supply all needs. He will cut through the hotel lobby to save thirty seconds.

He marches through the revolving door and into the dense memories of the next hour of his life. His mind spins, as he reconstructs fading in-and-out images, everything at once, to be reassembled and recombined. He struggles to focus on the bare events, to purge insinuating passions. He must see the entire mobile landscape before lying memory edits his experience, pares it down to its own version, and erases the rest. He kneads his eyes and focuses past the angel chandelier on the hotel's cracked ceiling at which, unseeingly, he has stared. He notices the hotel bedroom wallpaper for the first time, that the light gray fleurs-de-lis alternate with yellow ones. The same pattern Odile and he pasted to the wall near their marriage bed on the sixth floor of the apartment building on rue d'Anglais. Fleurs-de-lis jolt him awake into memory. How had he missed the exact same fleurs-de-lis earlier tonight? But fleurs-de-lis pervade. The masculine little flower-cum-spearheads have been ubiquitously French since the Middle Ages. He did not see fleurs-de-lis for the same reason he missed the sign in the window yesterday. All is central now, only the sidewalks and shaving cream are peripheral. Neither did he notice that the second lock on his apartment door was not latched. Nor did he see the two belted brown leather bags in the lobby with La Plata stickers on them. Were he more sensitive, less preoccupied, more attentive, less self-absorbed, he would have distinguished signals, very clear signals, from noise. He would have anticipated the obvious possibilities. He would have acted to avoid shock.

Signs displayed in hotel windows: American Manufacturers' Association, Nov. 25–27. Welcome. Traffic Engineers of New England and Mid-Atlantic States Convention Friday noon until Saturday 6 PM. Instituto Pan Americano de Neurocirujanos y Neuroanatomistas, Nov. 25–Dec. 1. He enters the airlock of the door, relieved to be out of the wind. His nose drips; don't forget shaving cream and he'd better buy tissues and nasal spray too. He runs his hands along his chapped ears on the way toward the drugstore.

Enjoying the overheated lobby as he crosses toward the Fourteenth Street exit, he sees the back of an attractive figure facing a tall, red-headed man and gesturing to a small, bald man on the left. The three are waiting in the reception desk line to check in. Six pieces of luggage stacked neatly like a child's fortress. Two unequal-sized matched strapped bags off to the side bear "La Plata, Universidad de La Plata" and "Paraná" stickers. Georges starts with recognition. It is his baggage. Good, stout, warm brown leather matching cases, each with a single brass-buckled belt and two zippers. Well-worn now, but of high quality, and unmistakable.

As he draws closer, his heartbeat quickens. Georges calculates his rate of approach, a pace per second, and notes his trajectory. He cannot cross the lobby without passing within two meters of her. She turns to laugh at something the short man says. He sees her brown eyes still shine. Her chin has its plum-cleft, a little riper than he remembers. She has no gray hair. She has hardly changed except for deeper laugh wrinkles near the eyes. Was he seeing her now, or had he somehow found her, finally, as she was? He is vertiginously disoriented. What are the facts of his life? Where—*when* is he? How long has it taken for him to come here to this precise point?

This excess of emotional energy burns his chest. He wants to quantify it: his heartbeats double, his temperature rises, the breathing is quick, shallow—he slows his pace. He refuses to lower his head, to scurry past Argentinian surgeons and Brazilian anatomists. Refusing to evade he quickly sees that the three friends, old colleagues, are comfortable with each other. She cannot miss Georges. Any moment now. What will he do? Shall he ask her why she is not dead? Why did she leave? Why did she abandon a happy sweet three-year-old? Will she recognize him? What does she know about his life? About Alain now? Will he talk?

Attempts to quantify dissolve. He is seized by a fury to comb his hair. He seeks a mirror, a reflective window, it is a hotel lobby for chrissake. He absolutely must know right now how old he looks. He sees himself in a flaking mirror surrounded by fleurs-de-lis, naked and twenty-five, as behind him she bends for something he can't see.

Is his nose red? Can she see it still dripping? At a pace per second, it is becoming too late. Georges sniffs, thrusts a sweaty hand in his pocket for his handkerchief. She looks up at the sniffle as if he had called her name. He feels a gentle shiver; his heart slows, breath catches for a moment. She looks deep into his eyes. Familiarity first, then compassion. Warmth actually. She must be fifty-five now; how can it be that she still, with a mute smile, moves him so?

He, directly before them, steps into handshake range. He knows now he is revealed, every wrinkle and gesture, though her eyes do not leave his. The prattle ceases. She stops mid-sentence, the chattering to her colleagues fades. She waits calmly, unperturbed. *"Bonsoir,* Georges," she says.

"Bonsoir, Odile," he answers; *"adieux."* He continues walking on schedule.

He was not aware of any decision. He had simply maintained the preplanned schedule. He buys an economy-size bottle of floral shampoo for his leather shaving case. He does not pose any questions; the only real question left is not his to ask. He hands the sales clerk a hundred-dollar bill. He feels a release of sadness and hope long-held. His pride stings, but his guilt pervades, exudes from the skin and foams from the mouth. He feels a lingering warmth, sweetened with nostalgia. He chides himself for the childishness of the erection he feels as he pockets his change.

That ancient decision of hers precluded consultation; it was nonnegotiable. Maybe, too, it was the least cruel way for Alan, and ultimately the most generous and wise. She knew, with her serious, quiet determination, that she could not change Georges. He remembers she walked infant Alain night after night. He remembers the evening she missed a lecture by some famous French neuroanatomist. Georges, home from the lab exhausted, found her in tears, because he failed to come home on time, at the time he said he would.

Georges, packages in hand, does not even feel the cold wind at the nape of his neck, shepherding him back to his apartment. He turns his key in the lock, bumps the still-closed door, fiddles the key back. Something is wrong. He enters bemusedly. A chair is overturned, showing its nude white underside. The bed is gaping at him. Phonograph records tile his floor; the turntable is caught in a web of strings from his wall map. Has he been robbed? Thieves don't bother with your old records. . . . A bang and sudden footsteps panic him; he drops his package and spins to find Maria Elena stumbling from the bathroom, damp black hair flopping like a wig, her makeup an avalanche down her cheeks, her eyes flashing. She holds out a whorl of little yellow papers like baby chicks and throws them at him. As he cowers and grabs at a couple, automatically looking for written justification, she hurls an ashtray at him, which misses and bounces off the drywall behind him.

"What's wrong? Please tell me what's wrong." Looking into her dark eyes he sees only the tearful young Odile. He blinks, startled back into the present and eager to leave. He glances at of his Italian watch: 5:30. He has to be at Kennedy by 7 p.m. He needs to leave *now*—not soon, *now*. "Please, dear, tell me what's wrong." Maria Elena sobs. She sniffles. She moans. Could he risk packing the things he has just bought and closing his suitcases, without first relieving the pain of her out-burst? "Come, Maria Elena, tell me first what's wrong, please, please. You know I must leave in a few moments."

She gnashes her teeth and nods at the papers strewn about the floor, the bed, the tables. "See," she said, "look at those,"—her soft voice very Mexican now—"and that's not all," she goes on. "I come to tell you something—that's why I come today. . . . I'm pregnant, and it is by you."

He looks in her face. She is betrayed. She feels she does have a right to him, is that it? He wants to question her, but she looks desperate. He realizes she is in earnest. He picks up one of the papers. Dozens of little yellow slips all from his telephone notepad are scattered here and beyond. They had fallen like leaves about his feet. He gathers a handful slowly.

"They is all over," she says, "in the bed, in the bathroom, on the floor, in the kitchen, everywhere. Who is Denise?"

Some are in French, some in English. He shuffles through the first ten. "Georges, I still feel your balls where they ought to be, next to me. Georges, it is très facile to be lewd in English, I lust for your male parts. Georges, let us go together on the shuttle, it would be a marvelous place to fuck. Next week in France I'll open up my legs for you. Georges, je t'aime—plus que tous les autres hommes que j'ai connus. I close my eyes and you appear in my arms, nipples to nipples. Georges, c'est vrai, there are certain things you do even better than my husband, come and do them again with me. It is too bad I love you so much and you love me so little and that we are both too old. Next weekend I'll be in Paris at the Hotel rue St. Severin from Thurs. Telephonez-moi, STP. At the beginning of the week in Liège. We'll arrange something. Twice a year is not sufficient. I need you."

"Maria Elena," he says calmly, "Mme Professeur Dr. Denise LeClerc is a colleague and a friend. She is Professor of Space Science in the Department of Astronomy at the University of Liège—in Belgium! I hardly ever see her. Don't worry about her. She thinks she loves me but she'll get over it." 5:44.

Maria Elena wipes her eyes. "I'm pregnant, Georges, he is your baby. Can't you please marry me? We can have him. I'm strong. I'll take care of everything."

Georges closes his eyes to think. He sees Odile looking into him with her brown eyes, even as she holds his suitcase with the La Plata sticker on it. He rubs his face with one hand and pink phosphenes reveal Mme LeClerc's nipples. He opens his eyes to see the real Maria Elena's face. He must leave or he will miss the plane, the talk, his Monday morning presentation. Marry Maria Elena? He is may still be married to Odile! He now wonders—where did I stash the probable annulment and likely death certificate?

He takes Maria Elena's hand gingerly. The tears cease to spring and well below her red-shot, widening eyes. "No, Maria Elena," he says slowly, "we are not going to be married. I will never marry again. I'm not fit for marriage. I would ruin your life, and you have all of it in front of you. You can have the baby, if you wish, but I think it would be better not to. Whatever you choose to do, I'll help you however I can. Don't worry. I must go right now, but I'll be back in two weeks."

"Two weeks!" she wails. "I know damn well you go to France to fuck Madame! I know everything you do together, you son-of-a-bitch!"

He finishes packing while she sobs. He hefts his bags and turns to her in the doorway. "Please put this place into some order before you go and double-lock the door. I must go or I'll miss my plane."

"Go on, you fuck!" she cries. "Who needs you? I don't. No one does, not even Madame!" Her breath catches, and she exhales, then says quietly, "You're useless. You just fuck and go on with yourself, like a peasant. Forget two weeks; go away forever. Go to Hell. Adios. Good-bye." She gently pushes his lapels with both hands, putting him out of her way, and walks out. He hears the sharp, regular clack of her heels, all the way down the stairwell and then down the doorsteps before the outer door closes.

He regrets all the way to the airport that he has left his apartment in a mess for two weeks. He thinks about calling his mother in New Jersey. He'll ask her to clean it up for him. No, bad idea—she reads French. He boards his plane as they are closing the doors only because he does not stop once.

He sits up and moves off the papers hiding the bed. He steps back to the window. The church bells are ringing still, or is it again? A memorial, or a *fête*? Few cars now, shops and apartments darkened, only the city lights and the shine of rain on the street below revealing Paris. His mind empties. He absorbs the slick slate-tiled rooftops. He returns to this place for the first time. He must sleep. He must begin to sleep this minute in the brevity of darkness.

He will have to leave no later than eight o'clock to arrive at Concord-Lafayette on time. How will he find anyone, French or not, to cover the cost of the Spacelab if he fails to sleep now? How will he ever make any sense of the facts and schemata in the manuscript at the bed? He lies across the untouched piles. Who will help him present his case? He absolutely must sleep. Has he driven all his women away? Perhaps not Denise. Maybe she still loves him. He will call her in Liège—maybe he won't even have to. She may be sitting there in the audience tomorrow, appreciating his

French, calculating the projected budgets, responding to his pleas for action, understanding his nuances, planning to help him raise the French contribution to the Spacelab. She probably has been invited to the joint ESA panel meeting. Yes, it's all very likely. He will see. On this thought, Georges slips into sleep.

MEETING

Those who handled sciences have been either
men of experiment or men of dogmas. The
men of experiment are like the ant, they only
collect and use; the reasoners resemble spiders
who make cobwebs out of their own substances. . . . Therefore from a closer and purer
league between these two faculties, the experimental and the rational (such as has never yet
been made), much may be hoped.

Francis Bacon, 1561–1626
Novum organum p. 46 in *The Nature of Life*
Readings in Biology,
The Great Books Foundation, Chicago, 2001

COSPAR, as outer space aficionados know, stands for
Committee on Space Research. The biennial week-long congress is so labor-intensive that more than a single professional
service and many volunteers are required to organize it.
COSPAR congresses since the first was launched in 1960 have
gone to Azerbaijan (Armenia), Mainz (W. Germany), Orleans
(northern France), San Sebastian (Basque country of Spain),
Wakulla Springs in Florida, Tokyo, and Hong Kong, among
other places. Perusal of the poorly maintained records show
that COSPAR will go wherever at least one internationally
known entrepreneurial scientist has coaxed at least one ambitious businessman and several scientific colleagues to lead the
action. It is crucial that the key scientist in his own country
convince someone with a bevy of secretaries and a vague or

uncommitted budget to be willing to attend to the minutiae of detail. Organizational meetings to set the site four years in the future begin the process. The scientist and his political allies must draw out their plans in conciliatory committee meetings held at least two years ahead. Immediately after each international meeting the COSPAR heavies plot for the new location. The space scientists jostle for authority over the meeting four years hence. Any man who speaks clearly and loudly, who enjoys a professional address and an unblemished scientific record, and who really *wants* the onerous two-three-tedious-year task of organizing the never-fully-reimbursed week-long congress more or less may have it.

The self-selected international organizers in 1996 opted for a single theme in 1999: "revival of manned space flight by 2010." Specialists insisted they be included: rocket engineers, cosmologists, and gravitational biologists. Graduate students envisioned generating interest for their arcane studies, every proponent of each of the planets and satellites in the solar system demanded equal time. Europa and Titan enthusiasts requested a full morning session each. They argued for excellent chances of life outside the Earth. Taken together, requests for nearly one hundred simultaneous sessions were brought to the table. Based on past attendance, even in Washington, the most popular tourist destination in the world, no COSPAR meeting had ever boasted more than 1,500 attendees. When Girard Beaumont loudly asserted that each session would probably attract an audience of only ten to fifteen people, passionate voices defended the decision to permit a large number of simultaneous sessions.

The magnitude of the task and a measly $10,000 grant

from NASA combined with an equal amount from ESA (the European Space Agency) brought the COSPAR monster to Washington. Georges Standon, in a move that did not surprise anyone, was unanimously voted chair of the entire Congress. Howard Fein, dean of the Roosevelt Medical School in Chicago, was assigned the task of assessing the effect of the outer space environment on the long-term travel (three years to Mars and back) of cosmo-astronauts. In 1997, when Dr. Fein's services were solicited by the Washington COSPAR secretariat, the Argentine anatomist Odile Bustamonte had been a visiting professor on Michigan Avenue in Roosevelt's Department of Neuroscience and Behavior for an entire year. Because her office was near Fein's, they had met casually at several lunches with mutual friends. Dr. Fein exercised his chairmanship prerogative and asked her to put together a morning session to be named "Manned Space Flight-Physiology in Space," a panel of no more than four speakers.

Georges Standon asked his French colleagues, at an ESA meeting in 1996—he always prepared in advance—who might be qualified to help assess the air quality and pressure in any space ship or planetary landing, on, say, Mars. By two different colleagues Georges was given Raoul Gautier's name, on a small folded piece of paper and an index card, both of which he stuffed in his pockets. One was lost when he took the pants for cleaning, the other went through the washing machine and dripped ink on his shirt. But when both Denise LeClerc and then Alton Brainard also gave him the name of Raoul Gautier at the 1997 meeting of the meteoritic impact subcommittee, he remembered. Remembering, he decided to act. After he phoned Steve Ramsey, his mind was made up to invite Gautier to chair the "atmospheric gases" session even though he had never laid eyes on the man. Gautier, in spite of bygones, invited René Schiller (René Pemberlain Schiller) to join his panel.

No one recorded how it happened, but during a coffee break at the first COSPAR plenary session, René met a woman who needed help in the ladies' lavatory at the Hilton hotel because someone had failed to replace the rolls of toilet paper in all three stalls. That solved, René who had taken the other's accent as French, introduced herself. When René read the woman's name tag, she recognized the name to be Spanish: Odile Bustamonte. One fast comment lead to the next. They were lodged on the same floor in the same wing so that, the following morning Odile invited René to join her for breakfast and told her exactly when, for how long and how well she had known Georges Standon. She confessed remorse, but not embitterment. As women will but men won't, whether scientists or not, Odile began to talk. She explained the circumstances of the birth and the continued existence of Alan (Alain) Standon. She mentioned that, through Grandma Barbara, without Georges's knowledge, she sent him money, received yearly photos and good news of her one son. René felt a surge of affection for this like soul: dark hair that had not been "hairdressed," perhaps not ever, and a face showing both laugh lines and intellectual acuity. Odile, not necessarily shy with strangers in different fields whom, it was likely, she would never see again, talked fast and exuded impatience. This style, its lilting accent, added to the scientific literacy and endeared her even more to René.

Breakfast over, the coffee gone, and the meetings about to start more than a block away, René decided that Odile's confidence ought to be rewarded in kind. She beamed with calm pride. Out of character for her, she nearly bragged. She blurted out about how happy she was in her marriage to Randall Schiller. He studied history and was both a diplomat and a musician. Not, that is, *not a scientist*. How fulfilling was their life together after her wounds: the four-year fiasco with atmospheric chemist Raoul Gautier. Sure, Raoul had been probably her only true (but utterly impossible) love and possibly her only true (and utterly marvelous) colleague. But things with them were always problematic, whereas with Schiller they were simply good—except for the one disconcerting fact of her own reproductive biology.

Five years and a whole lot of money had been spent attempting pregnancy by in vitro. Nothing seemed to work. How she and Randall Schiller (Rando to his friends) wanted their own children; his sperm count was healthy but apparently the botched abortion was to blame. So long ago, so distant when she was oh, so young, apparently whatever happened had left her sterile even though the gynecologists couldn't really see why she should be. She didn't blame Howard Fein now, she never had. She was equally to blame, wasn't she. René was even more naïve than he in those student days before she became a chemist. Her health had always been good. She really never even noticed her childlessness until most of her friends had kids and busy lives that curtailed their scientific and social activities. Only at that point did René realize she was not only ready but maybe even overripe for them.

Oh well, there are too many kids in the world anyway,

aren't there, and she and Rando did enjoy the freedom of their lives. In fact, she loved her professional and personal activities too much to even consider adoption of anyone else's children! She loved her science. She loved her students. Her students, after all, were her kids. No pregnancies, no diapers, no kitchen slavery, and lots of adult conversation.

The science to her, from Chicago and Yale to COSPAR biennials, continues to become broader and more interesting. Space science has recognized its deepening need for not only chemistry but gas emissions by bacteria and other forms of life. The problems in space sciences have transformed; they are more closely defined. Her task is so much more creative, more compelling and lively as she became associated with the branch of physical science now called "atmospheric chemistry," ever more a recognized field. Atmospheric chemistry is international, it has to be, and it is a better funded field now that it has moved far beyond meteorology and entirely abandoned weather prediction.

René smiled. She said thoughtfully, "Science will go on. Men come and go, men will come and go but science, life itself, will always go on." Odile responded, "Science is always a continuation. Sure. Clearly. René, I know I do know you for all of my whole life. At the banquet tomorrow we must project to sit together. I could not care if Raoul Gautier or Howard Fein or even both two will be there. Indeed, it might even be more fun if both assisted." "Of course," said René, "Let's plan on it, sounds like a great idea to me. Lots of fun. I'd love it. *A demain*, then."

"Nice to meet you," they both said so quickly, yet simultaneously. They each paid the cashier and hurried off to their respective scientific sessions, determined not to be late. The same fleeting thought probably now amused them both as well. Except for scientific collegiality, the renewal of old friendships, and even very occasionally, the making of new friends, those inevitable banquets at the ends of meetings are tedious, expensive, caloric bores.

SUNDAY MORNING WITH
J. ROBERT OPPENHEIMER

Turning and turning in the widening gyre
The falcon cannot hear the falconer;
Things fall apart; the centre cannot hold;
Mere anarchy is loosed upon the world,
The blood-dimmed tide is loosed, and everywhere
The ceremony of innocence is drowned;
The best lack all conviction, while the worst
Are full of passionate intensity.

William Butler Yeats
"The Second Coming"

September 1986

As the men talked quietly, I imagined Kaori, my college roommate's aunt. The family chronicle was recounted by her uncle: the deaths of his wife and daughter. Aunt Kaori, he said, had groped for her baby who had slipped away from her, but she could not move because only stumps and cascades of dark blood remained where her legs had been. Her slippery child, still trying to scream as charred black peeled off her cheek, died. Kaori managed to touch its thigh. Like Kaori and her daughter, one hundred thousand others perished instantly after that first moment. And like my roommate's surviving uncle, many more were never again entirely alive.

We were seated comfortably in Cambridge—surrounded by large format atlases printed in Italy, origami miniatures (cranes, butterflies, squares) strewn on the floor, and the clutter of a too-ample late supper—talking about Hiroshima, about that day forty-one years before. Despite my vivid images of Aunt Kaori, I was listening intently and more quietly than I usually do. David Hawkins, my friend, and Phil Morrison, our host, were reliving it again, Morrison grimacing. Hawkins, philosopher and educator, Los Alamos veteran, was the author of the official history of the making of the bomb. His self-accusations of pedantry and churlishness in his own writing—a solicited report so detailed he claimed it was unintelligible even to him—did not take the catch out of his voice as he spoke.

I had heard of Professor Morrison long before meeting him. Thirty years earlier my then boyfriend, Carl Sagan, an aspiring scientist, had told me more than once: "Morrison armed Fat Man at Tinian." Tinian was the island in the South Pacific from which the atom bomb to Japan was flown, Fat Man the nickname of the bomb: Morrison, Carl claimed, had helped load the bomb onto the plane.

As if mocking how finite the post-Apollo, plate-tectonic Earth had become, a three-dimensional globe—on a turntable pedestal, lighted from within—cast shadows over us. I fixed upon the mid-Atlantic ridge, visible on the glowing planet.

Phil and David were remembering arguments with the great leader whose passion it had been to build the bomb: J. Robert Oppenheimer. The issue was whether or not to deploy Fat Man—whether or not, after the bomb had been successfully developed and tested, to drop it.

Phil looked through me. "Oppenheimer wanted to drop it; he felt it *must* be dropped. It was his Fat Man, his son, his invention. But not his alone—it was not his possession, rather his shared glory. It was living proof that all the esoterica, all the equations, all the arcane formulas and the ineffable mystery were something. Something tangible. Something of economic and political value."

He paused, neatly cracking open an almond shell with a table knife. "All the effort, the great quantities of money, were worth it. Our activities were not just the poetry of meaningless mathematics. For nearly three years Oppenheimer labored ceaselessly; with him, for him, we worked as hard. It was our labor of love. After all, we were stopping carnage in Europe, the destruction of civilization, the Hitler madness. We had the means to make the difference. Of course, Oppie argued we cannot just *have* the bomb. We must *drop* the bomb."

Phil ate the almond.

"I was such an idiot. I admired Robert Oppenheimer. He was of course my senior and my superior. It would be presumptuous to say I loved him or even feared him—Oppenheimer filled me with angst. Whatever the case, I listened to him. He had many arguments." Phil ticked them off. "We had the most dangerous weapon in the history of mankind. This A-bomb was qualitatively different; it wasn't just more TNT. The A-bomb could generate apocalypse. It absolutely had to be contained by common consent. But how could the public restrain a monster they could not even imagine? We were responsible for public display of the A-bomb. We must unequivocally demonstrate the enormity of potential devastation." He paused.

"We had to end all war. We *could* end all war. Therefore, the bomb had to be dropped in an unequivocal manner—there must be thousands of eyewitnesses to its destructiveness."

We were silent as the shadows continued to spin.

"I agreed with Oppenheimer," Phil was nodding, slowly. "I wanted to drop the bomb to reveal indiscriminate horror; I was sure my fellow man would end war. All sane people, including even the most dedicated military men, would see that war where one bomb could obliterate New York or Paris was unthinkable. At first we had paper calculations proving that a single detonation might even burn the air itself, the potential conflagration of the entire atmosphere. OK, they were proved incorrect . . . the probability of burning air was vanishingly low. Still, I was nagged for years by a persistent nightmare of the final whole-Earth bonfire.

"Who was I? A young physics student. Very close to the action and passionately interested but, as usual, overassessing my own importance. Inspired by my own sense of moral imperative I spoke out with the assurance of the young. We met nearly every night then—any scientist or technician could come, and, of course, I always went feeling swept away by the big fact that we were making history. I always spoke up, even then. I insisted on a public A-bomb explosion. I knew Oppenheimer was right, we must demonstrate the power to as many military people from as many places as possible. This explosion—the very fact of it—would reveal how ludicrous was the continuation of weapons development. But I suggested a well-publicized display of the bomb in the Pacific Ocean. I felt President Truman should invite not only allies but Japan and Germany. I found out, only later of course, that I was far from alone in advocating a grand public demonstration.

"Oppie vehemently opposed demonstration. He had been emphatic as soon as the bombs were ready: 'For us to stop all war, we have to stop this war now.' We must launch a surprise attack. We must demolish a significant Japanese military target. Even after Germany's surrounder it was not enough. We need the immediate surrender of Japan. Oppie had said spookily, I remember it so clearly: 'We must *use* Fat Man. We must bomb Berlin and Tokyo simultaneously.'"

Phil held the pedestal, spinning the lighted globe hard, throwing shadows. He cracked another almond.

"Why do you say you were such an idiot?" David asked.

Phil looked, distracted, past David, past me, past the globe. "After weeks of pondering, arguing, and debating we were all just about agreed: General Leslie Groves, the other physicists, everyone, even the wives—but mostly Oppie. Once we knew the bombs would work we all met. We listened to Oppie that night after supper, in the big hall. The idea was," he held up his fingers:

"One, we must drop the bomb to show the world its power—to end war.

"Two, we'd drop it on Japan first, on as strictly a military target—like Hiroshima or Nagasaki—as we could find. If Japan did not surrender immediately after Fat Man was deployed, then our have a contingency plan was to hit Germany afterward with the second bomb. As it happened Germany surrendered first.

"Three, we must drop the A-bomb as soon after testing as possible.

"There were only a few remaining questions. How much prior notice should the world be given that the bomb attack was real and inevitable? Who should be notified? The entire literate world? How much earlier? An ultimatum should be issued first I thought and at the very least, some time must be left for evacuation.

"And I was an idiot. In the beginning I argued, I wanted to see as much publicity beforehand as possible. In the end, I was for no notification of anyone. I was an idiot."

"Why?" David asked.

"I let one argument sway me," Phil was nodding again, "an argument to which I never should have listened. Can you guess what it was that convinced me to let us go ahead and drop the bomb with no prior notice?"

David answered, "Probably no one listened to you because Oppenheimer—in his typically ambivalent way—wanted to feel the full power of the moment: the bomb released at a target and on a schedule to which only he was privy. You were too young anyway, who would listen to you?"

Phil shook his head. "Yes, I was young but that wasn't it. I don't think Oppenheimer was such a power-seeker. That wasn't it. It was the crew. It was all about the American crew—I knew the pilot: Tibbets."

"What do you mean the crew? Who is Tibbets?" David asked softly. I held my breath.

"They pointed out—Oppie, Groves, and others—that if we gave any notice at all we would be rightly accused of murdering the crew. If warned, the enemy defense would get ready; the plane delivering the bomb would surely be shot down. They'd be dead, sacrificed. The crew would become a rallying cry, scapegoats of physicists' whims. There were, in fact, several potential pilots. All had the requisite technical training. Two or three had been at Los Alamos for years with us; I knew them all by sight.

"But Tibbets I knew best. One of his sons was already a superb pianist with an ambition to compose. I thought about the inevitable death of the father. I ended up agreeing to a secret bombing. I thought I was saving this pilot's life. One life against one hundred thousand."

Pain showed through Phil's eyes. David looked away.

"But if you had another chance," David asked, "what would you have done—if you knew what you know now? You were only twenty-nine then, after all. What would you have decided?"

"I don't know." There were shadows in Phil's face. "I do not know. The public still does not understand. No one fathoms the seriousness of these weapons. Sometimes I still think we need more demonstrations—not in New York City or Washington, D.C., but say in Fairfax County, Virginia, or Bethesda, Maryland. Or here on the Cambridge Common, Westchester County, or Grosse Point, Michigan."

He paused. "I'm not seriously advocating bombing residential areas. In fact, I guess if I had it all to do over, I'd end up listening to Oppie again. He conceived the project, he brought us together to work like demons, he inspired us with the physics, he exuded ambience—it was his sweet victory. At that moment, I trusted his wisdom. It wasn't just loyalty to my leader. It was that J.R.O. was sage. I still believe he believed his goal was to stop Hitler in particular and war in general. Yes," Phil's voice was sadly certain, "Yes, I probably would just support Oppenheimer again."

We dispersed shortly after, serious conversation reverting

to the superficial as we descended the stairs—boom in health food sales of *Spirulina*, bacteria sold under the safe, plant-sounding name of "blue-green algae."

As we entered the sudden evening chill, I remembered, first with clarity—Aunt Kaori's charred daughter—and then, joltingly, my version of J. Robert Oppenheimer. Oppie, the man who had changed the world in ways he never knew and could never have predicted. Until this conversation at the Morrisons', I had forgotten what I knew, thought I knew, of Professor Oppenheimer. A long winding of years, indeed, separated 1986 from 1955. I, too, had admired Oppenheimer.

> The hand that signed the paper felled a city;
> Five sovereign fingers taxed the breath,
> Doubled the globe of dead and halved a
> country;
> These five kings did a king to death.

> "The Hand that Signed the Paper"
> Dylan Thomas, 1936

March 1955

I was literally sophomoric and had just turned sixteen. The winter quarter at the University of Chicago had just ended; schoolwork finished was a great relief. Overassessing my talents, unconscious of my self-centeredness, I was convinced that great insights were revealed in my latest brilliant paper: "Not 'Whether or Not?' but 'How?'—J. Robert Oppenheimer and the Decision to Drop the Atomic Bomb."

Of all the pages of analyzed quotations, Oppie's 1954 statement kept playing in my mind.

> It is my judgment in these things that when you see something that is technically feasible you go ahead and do it and argue about what it is only after you have had your technical success. That is the way it was with the atomic bomb. I do not think anybody opposed making it, there were some debates about what to do with it after it was made.

My boyfriend, one of many, coaxed my company for his spring-break trip East. The Princeton campus—a place I had always wanted to visit—was, he urged, only 900 miles from Chicago. Looked at another way, it was only half an hour drive to Rahway, New Jersey, Carl's home town. Reluctant to drive thirty hours alone, Carl was equally ambivalent about taking me the final thirty minutes to Rahway. He wanted to avoid the inevitable flurry were he to arrive home with a young woman.

Carl, less sophomoric than I, enjoyed an exaggerated sense of his own importance. He had only superficially understood Copernicus's lessons: Galileo's idea had been taken in logically but not emotionally. Despite centuries of thought succeeding Ptolemy, my aspiring astronomer functioned as though the Earth (Rahway in particular) were the dead center of the universe. His mother, incessantly orbiting around her son, would ask unanswerable questions:

"Where did you sleep on the road?"

"What are your intentions toward your young lady friend?"

"Are you going to interrupt your studies?"

"What kind of family does she come from that they permit her to travel such a long distance with a young man—unaccompanied?"

"Do they have money?"

"What does her father do?"

Resolved, I was invited, but not quite for the distance. Nevertheless, I assented, out of Princeton curiosity and Carl lust. Leaving on a mid-March Friday night, we shared the burden of the drive: Indiana, Ohio, and, especially trying, Pennsylvania's interminable new turnpike. Finally, Princeton, New Jersey; with a peck on the lips, Carl dropped me at the Nassau Tavern and accelerated, alone and unembarrassed, homeward.

To pay for the Nassau Tavern, I carefully counted out money from meager after-school earnings. Since September I had set up pins in a bowling alley for the women's physical education classes. Counting out the bills, I could hear smooth balls echoing down shiny alleys and shocked pins bouncing.

The tavern was not pompous. As Aunt Kaori's husband would say, it was *shibui*—studied, quiet elegance; shibui in a familiar Yankee American way.

It was dusk when I settled into the spare, comfortable, maple-furnished room. I telephoned home. As expected, my father answered—he hated Saturday night crowds so had made going out only on Fridays part of his religion. I tried my plan on him: "I'm in Princeton. I'm thinking of visiting J. Robert Oppenheimer."

"Do it!" Pa responded straightaway. "Now is the time.

You may never have another chance. Tell him you admire him." Pa was excited. "Tell him—now that he's been put down, now the publicity's faded, tell him lots of us respect him. Do it now," he shouted with characteristic enthusiasm. "He's Jewish, too, you know. At least," the slow sigh, "he used to be. That's what making waves does to *Yekehs*." (My father, not without a tinge of envy, always called German Jews, whom he supposed to be his cultural—but not genetic—superiors, Yekehs). "Go on—it's now or never. Go see him, Lynnie. Now. You'll never have a chance again."

The media had tired of Oppenheimer. Maybe because the public had villainized him, I thrilled at every mention of him. His history, the irony of his life's work, the extraordinary blue eyes all fascinated me.

Did he have trouble sleeping at night? Could he have sensed at all, worrying through theoretical equations, that their application would lead, finally, not only to his own fall but to the destruction of thousands of people? Was it as clichéd as climbing a mountain because it's there? Could it possibly be human nature to do what the tools enabled, the "technologically sweet," no matter what the consequences? Was Dr. Oppenheimer, as he grappled in Los Alamos, thinking of the stinking meat smell of gassed Jewish flesh; was he trying to stop the Nazis? Or was he just glorying in the chance to push his intelligence to its limits? What did he believe; rather, what did he believe he believed?

Oppenheimer's story obsessed me. Could I ever lose myself like he did? I loved science, could I ever hunt and then be haunted by its applications, forgetting about the knowledge in and for itself?

By March 1955, Oppenheimer's fame had metamorphosed in a way I could imagine terrifying to such a public person. He did not matter any more. No one cared. The FBI had accumulated voluminous files for many years; then, abruptly, "case closed." He might as well have been dead. The man revered as an American hero, then beaten by scandals, had retreated, withdrawn from the public eye.

The weather when I awoke was delicious—cold, bright. I still remember the distinct brown and yellow sunbeams, the sweet smells of eastern spring as I gazed across Palmer Square from my second-story window. Just as the man selling newspapers blew into his cupped hands, I saw the headline printed in red: "We Meet the Oppenheimers."

The "Dear Readers" column, by Dorothy Schiff, columnist and owner of the *Post,* took the front page, an attempt to wring some news from a case closed since the previous summer. Schiff was "surprised to hear Mrs. Oppenheimer," the German-born "femme fatale" who had led a dramatic life, "speak American so well." "She sounded," Schiff crooned, " . . . like a Park Avenue socialite; her face shows the ravages of strong emotion rather than time." Katharine Oppenheimer reminded Schiff of a "flaming youth" of the 1920s; a heroine in an F. Scott Fitzgerald novel "capable of romantic and reckless action." And Oppie, "with his wide mouth and liquid blue eyes looked like a man who had been crying, but . . .

> I think he is too aloof, too disdainful, too philosoph-
> ical to indulge in self-pity. Something about his ears
> and the way he moved reminded me of a fawn.

Perhaps he is more like a chameleon. . . . That afternoon he was not the frustrated fanatic I had seen on
the Murrow program, the abstruse poet I had heard
on a Columbia University broadcast, nor the trapped
scientist-turned-politician who emerged from the
testimony. . . . Someone at the luncheon had asked
Oppenheimer if he thought the H-bomb would ever
be used. For the first time he laughed, but not mer-
rily. "Only a sphinx could answer that," he said,
adding something about the bomb's "limited use,"
which, to my dismay, he seemed to advocate.

I grew angrier as I read. Schiff's article reflected both the
attitude of the public and their flagging interest in the
Oppenheimer case. It personified for me the society from
which he had withdrawn: prying eyes, vicarious thrills, superficial judgments, facile criticisms of what was not understood, patriotism and parochialism, fear of imagination and
culture, and abysmal, abysmal, ignorance of science.

What could Dorothy Schiff possibly know of science, of
love, of the too-human failure of judgment? At sixteen,
with my term paper conflicts and subtleties completed, I
clearly understood. He, personally, had had the power to
do something about stopping war and stopping Nazis.
Wasn't to play technologically, to explore and deploy, as
intrinsic to our nature as making love?

I put the *Post* away, ate breakfast, and then, simply, looked
up the address of Dr. Oppenheimer in the Princeton direc-
tory—Olden Lane. A short walk, five-minute hitchhike, and
a little local aid brought me to the Olden Lane street sign.

I scrutinized every house on the lane. The first faced another street, the second one too; I assumed they did not have Olden Lane addresses. The third house—charming, old, and weatherbeaten—directly across the wide lawn of the institute, seemed likely. No name at the door. In front on a fence a sign: "Drive Carefully Children Playing." The fourth had a name, not Oppenheimer. The garish, tiny fifth house looked improbable. The sixth had a name plaque. At the seventh I was approached by a menacing dog. The eighth looked too square and modern. I returned to the third house.

As I walked toward the front door I saw Dr. Oppenheimer, his wife, and two children coming toward me. I mumbled that I was here in Princeton. Studying science at college. Glad to see you, excuse me, just a minute—well—from Chicago, yes, yes. Glad to meet you. Going downtown—I, with you? Certainly, thank you.

Joining them in the white Cadillac convertible, I tried to sound modest as I boasted that I was the last of the liberal arts students to be graduating from The College under the Robert M. Hutchins A.B. plan. "You must be smart," said the son, Peter, born in August '41 and therefore just fourteen.

"Peter," Mrs. O. spoke slowly, too distinctly, "has just published his first article. It appeared in a column called 'Small Talk' in the television section of the university newspaper, *The Princeton*, with his byline." Silence.

"Oh," was the best I could do, not sure what to say. I wondered if Dr. O. felt as oppressed by his wife as I did.

We arrived at Palmer Square; I tagged along self-consciously. Mrs. O. looked in a shop window at Wedgwood china.

"That," I offered, "could not be Wedgwood; it has no wedges." She snapped a correction: "No, dear, I'm afraid you're wrong. I have bought Wedgewood sets several times without wedges."

Dr. O. went for tobacco and the newspaper, their ostensible reason for driving to town together every Sunday morning. There on the front page was Dorothy Schiff's "Dear Readers" with the dreadful banner. "We Meet the Oppenheimers—see page M7." I was embarrassed, for myself and for them, already feeling awkward in anticipation of the discussion it might provoke. I bought a carton of milk and walked across the street to drink it as Dr. O. and Peter were coming back. They waved. I offered pudgy Peter some milk, which he declined, saying that he only drank skim. My milk carton and I must look silly, I thought. When Dr. O. claimed he didn't mind, I realized I had said it aloud. "Harvard," he told me, "is a finer school than the University of Chicago."

"Robert, we need your help," Mrs. O. had opened the delicatessen door and was calling to us.

"Mine too?" I asked, not realizing the help was for choice of tobacco brand.

Peevish. "You needn't come in unless you like this store particularly."

I waited outside until Dr. O. joined me again in the street.

"About a month ago there was a screening of the longer version of the Murrow TV film about your work." I was enthusiastic, "Mandell Hall, the largest University of Chicago auditorium, filled up twice!"

His voice was contemplative, "Murrow's hour-and-a-half film interview gives an audience a better idea of the discussion, and even though the conversation, which lasted two hours, was cut, the film was much better than the forty-five minute TV show. But in both"—here he was emphatic—"the physics expositions that had had some continuity were lost on the audience. The cuts were unjust."

Then, he smiled. Those eyes looking directly at me, he asked warmly if I would like to come back to their home again. Mrs. Oppenheimer, coming out of the deli, overheard the invitation; she grimaced.

"Would I be disturbing you?"

She replied, a purposefully unmistakable tension in her voice, "Quite frankly, you'd be welcome only if you'd stay *just a little*. This is the only chance we have to be with the children, isn't it, Robert dear?"

"About twenty minutes," he added encouragingly and quietly so his remark went unnoticed by her. "Come, do come home with us, I have something to show you." I was delighted.

On the way back in that luxurious car we talked more about Murrow. The first time he had seen the finished TV film it had been in lovely surroundings. "The Murrows invited me up to their home; the poet and Abraham Lincoln biographer, Carl Sandburg, was there, also a guest. I had never met Sandburg before. He was very impressive. Sandburg is all that we generally think he is and more. . . . He also is a real man."

"Murrow?"

"No, Sandburg. Murrow is too, but Murrow is just like his television appearance; it reflects him accurately." Dr. O. went on, clearly talking directly to me.

Peter was sheepishly buried in the Sunday papers, hunkering down in the back seat with sullen Toni, the ten-year-old daughter. Although he's not more than two years younger than I am, he's a child and I'm an adult, odd. Peter, half under his breath, apologized for his dedication to the funny papers spread around him. "I'm not an intellectual type," he nodded as I scanned the Peter Rabbit he was reading.

Dr. O. handed me Peter's "Coming Attractions" column. "Peter is to be a regular contributor with a byline to the TV section." Mrs. O. interceded, audibly mumbling "unfair." She requested, rather fiercely, that I give her the paper.

Climbing out of the car, Dr. O. took my frowsy jacket and hurried to show me the thing he had promised. It was a Van Gogh original—a striking, colorful farm at sunset; the stars astonishing.

"This was part of my father's collection in San Francisco." He smiled wistfully and showed me another framed work, a pastel by a Frenchwoman, Belle Greene—was that the name of the person he mentioned? "I met the painter, a French contemporary of mine, not very well known. Greene died recently." Then, after he had examined with approval my large acetate scarf, tied and adjusted as a book sack—Harold Blum's thermodynamics book, *Time's Arrow and Evolution*, and a frayed, secondhand Kafka *Metamorphosis*—he showed me into the study.

"I apologize," he said, "for the sad state of my polylingual bookcase." There were academic German books, mostly mathematics, some French novels, and even a few Russian ones on the science shelves, a two-volume Chinese art set from

Taiwan, English and American poetry. He took up his pipe and opened a beer, obviously not his first of the day. He urged upon me a cigarette and whiskey or beer, which I refused. He pointed out books to me: a beautiful, handwritten, illustrated Blake. Another, Eric Bentley's *In Search of Theater*. "Bentley is a professor at Bennington and Rutgers. He works occasionally at the Institute," he explained, "we were classmates." His talk wandered dreamily.

I felt privileged.

"I've been at the Institute for seven years—I was in New Mexico during three of the war years. The name of this house is really Olden Manor. I just this week received a short-story collection—autographed," he added with a quick, proud smile, "from Carson McCullers."

"Is it *The Ballad of the Sad Café* by any chance?" I asked. "Yes, I think so." I told him I had read it and found it perfect, mythic. He asked me if I planned to write.

"How did you guess?" The question was silly, but it was already out of my mouth.

"Well—don't go to school for too long," he suggested, "and certainly don't go to study writing. You should go to Harvard." Then, as an aside, dryly, softly, and without much interest, he said to Mrs. Oppenheimer, "Kitty dear, you are not very entertaining."

She answered bluntly, "Well?"

"I imagine many people annoy you," I said, reserved.

"They do, they certainly do, don't they, darling?"

"You'd rather entertain your children, I'm sure," I said.

"We will, after you leave."

But then, Dr. O. said, "Oh, no. Do stay and eat with us."

He invited me with real feeling in his voice. He seemed sincerely to want me to stay.

"No, thank you very much"—it was hard, I was flattered—"but I'm not hungry now." Mrs. O. flashed him a triumphant smile.

Then, amid the tension that we all seemed to be feeling, we discussed the Schiff article. Dr. O. said that Mrs. Murray Kempton, whom they hardly knew, would feel more than he repercussions from the trumped-up "luncheon meeting" where the interview was conducted. "The conspirators usually suffer more than I when they are responsible for my bad press." He paused. "They usually are."

He and Mrs. Oppenheimer had accepted the invitation and agreed to the social lunch without any notion, of course, that a working reporter would be there. "Schiff maneuvered an interview by using her friends, Lloyd Garrison" (I had read that he was Dr. O.'s chief counsel) "and the *Post*'s editor, Murray Kempton. She obviously savored every minute of that contrived lunch visit, . . ." He hadn't felt betrayed, really, only impatient as if he were outside it, a spectator, perhaps, at a silly performance.

"I thought the article was stupid," I said.

"Yes," he went on. "I imagine it would seem confused and almost incoherent to the reader, although in fact it was just poor manners, crude."

Mrs. O. sat conspicuously reading the paper. With a sort of syncopated rhythm she kept glancing up at me. She eyed her watch, then glared forward into space. She looked harsh and determined. It was precisely 25 minutes since we had come in from the car; there was time for nothing more. Dr. O.

seemed to be dreaming, letting his thoughts unravel. Then, suddenly, noticing his wife's rigid posture, her eyes staring with intense, stifled impatience, he returned to alertness, not without revealing to me a twinge of regret.

"Well, good-bye," I said, politely shaking her hand. I turned to Dr. O. "It's been wonderful to meet you." He invited me, please, to come again soon—he must have guessed how I thrilled at his sincere invitation.

Furtively glancing at his tight-lipped wife (who was now, with some relief, leaning over the Sunday papers in concentration), he checked that she wasn't looking and smiled, warmly, deeply. He meant it; I tingled with pleasure. He shook my hand, gazed affectionately at me, then blankly at the street, with melancholy, gleaming blue eyes.

I walked back to the Nassau Tavern in a dream, wondering about my foray into the Oppenheimer family. I was certain that although Mrs. O. still resided with him, she had long since deserted him. She obviously did not share his interests, needs, nor aesthetic discernment; she clearly wanted no part of his battles with himself.

He had wanted me to stay. I had been permitted to catch a glimpse of, to feel the "intellectual sex appeal" that had attracted physicists to Los Alamos in 1943. He seemed like an aging stallion staggering from a broken spirit.

Did he ever think of Jean Tatlock? Had he ever, with his infamous antifascist love, enjoyed a relationship of a higher quality, a special plane of intimacy? Had he simply mismeasured Katharine's character, capabilities, during the exciting days of November 1940? Was her bitterness, the tension, the clash of wills, none of which either had made an effort to hide, all that was left between him and—as Dorothy Schiff had written—his "petite, chic, witty, tense, and vivacious" wife?

Had he felt a sense of failure or frustration or pity after all those years of pacing the corridors of power when, in the end, his security clearance, a symbol of his former influence, was denied? Was he left to feel it alone?

As I turned down Olden Lane drunk with Dr. O. and scents of spring, grinning with self-satisfaction and vanity, scarf with books tied over my shoulder, I easily convinced myself that I had known him better in that previous hour than Katharine had in all her years with him.

The adolescent euphoria receded; I had second thoughts. By the time I reached the hotel it began to come through to me. How brash to think that in one hour of invasion I could know anything at all. I thought of Schiff and her shabby article. I began to feel a bit ashamed. "You never know," a fellow student had said to me once as we were leaving class together, "you never know about couples unless you sleep under their bed." Still it had seemed to me then, and even does now, that Kitty and Oppie had lived days and years together in the same house but in separate worlds.

At the hotel I found a telephone message at the desk from Carl: "Please be packed and ready to leave by 3." I thanked the clerk and slowly climbed to my room, pondering my future. Should I consider marrying this cocksure scientist-to-be? Did I want a public life? Should I become a scientist's wife? Should I endure? Could I enjoy his certainty of future fame?

Of course, I'd ride back with him to Chicago, but I knew,

just then, I'd leave my New Jersey hero to his own imposing future. Dr. O. suggested I go to Harvard. Was he right? I contemplated Oppie's kind advice, "Don't go to school for too long, and certainly don't go to study writing."

Whatever his words, I learned far more from his example—the foils of his wife's eyes, the trapped desolation of his own. Yes, I would reassure Carl that he could enjoy the ease as he bloomed into a world-class scientist: he would never have to present me formally in Rahway. He would be eternally excused from ever introducing me to his mother.

As we sped west, a horizon of complexity lay before me.

Were those who failed to ask whether or not the bomb should be dropped to be blamed for the deaths of Hiroshima children?

Everyone had conceded that the building and detonation of the bomb was "technically sweet." Could J.R.O. have ceded his pleasure in the sweetness of how? Was it in the domain of the possible to demand, instead, that the bomb never be dropped? Could the "whether or not" question be asked at all? Did Oppie and his friends have only a single option?

All bomb systems were go. These weapons were unlike any in the history of warfare. No civilian, no sage elder, no mother, no child was exempt. Raging fires burn without distinguishing the armed soldier, the uniformed sailor, the dauntless marine.

> The darkness drops again; but now I know
> That twenty centuries of stony sleep
> Were vexed to nightmare by a rocking cradle,

And what rough beast, its hour come round
   at last,
Slouches toward Bethlehem to be born?

"The Second Coming"
William Butler Yeats

Feeling the undetectable spin of our planetary home, this globe, the Earth, I sky-gazed before mounting our own front steps. Incredible autumn stars. Bold, like his personal Van Gogh, the study for "Starry Night," Oppie so proudly had shown me, I had so proudly seen.

How ironic that on August 7, 1945, a hundred thousand Hiroshimi died at the hands of these superscientists whose only wish was to stop war forever, "It was his Fat Man, his son, his invention," Phil had said.

Is it ironic that today over fifty thousand nuclear fission weapons are tucked away in caves, in submarines, in ships' holds, in airplane payload bays? Or, had the desire to end all wars gone awash in the capability of doing something "technologically sweet," carrying on, asking no questions?

Was Oppenheimer correct or corrupting as he convinced a young Philip Morrison that a "mere demonstration" would not be enough? Settling that, that any warning to the Japanese would bring certain death to an American pilot, one death too many? It must be dropped over a populated area, it must be dropped with no warning. Sorting dark ironies with Kaori and all of those other human beings name-less, to us, now dead, is more difficult for me now than it was at age sixteen.

Orchestrating the project, Oppie became famous for his

"tendency to play ball" with the military, with the politicians, especially with the savvy and ambitious General Leslie Groves. Oppenheimer was mesmerized with the question "How?" never asking "Whether or not?" With pain, he later broadcast that he and his physicist colleagues had known sin. He stuttered. He halted. He raised issues of conscience. He debated Edward Teller, father of the next generation of bombs, mastermind of the H-bomb. "Wasn't the A-bomb enough?" Oppie questioned publicly. The turn of the screw, accusations at the '50s hearings—"Is he, with his sudden severe attack of conscience, standing in the way of progress?"

I am still the person I was at sixteen, perhaps more cynical, certainly more circumspect. Could I ever lose myself as Oppie did? My love for science—but not for scientists—has only deepened, as has my disdain for its applications. I see the touted use of any scientific insight for improvement of human health or military prowess as a profound distraction from the task to generate knowledge itself. So-called applied science—from molecular medicine miracles to hydrogen bomb detonations—is just more of the same talky-talky to thinly disguise greed: academic greed, scientist greed, corporate greed, government greed. Science is rationalized, confusion abounds, description obfuscated, havoc wreaked. Intrinsically hypocritical, unrecognized anthropocentrism breeds with itself, reducing exploration to snide self-justification. And then there are the victims, always the victims, the helpless-hopeless—the propaganda writers, the science journalists, the memorizing students, the part-time technicians, the lab rats and guinea pigs.

Yes, my enthusiasm for knowledge is unabated, while my

confidence in my fellow humans, especially fellow intellectuals, has eroded. Oppenheimer, the man, seems like the rest of them—far too accommodating, too malleable, too insubstantial, too indecisive to warrant serious reflection at this late date. Only, in some strange way, perhaps he, or at least the situation, *was* my mentor: the complex ambiguity of a persistent and vicious war, the Nazis and the disintegration of the great German culture, the racist comic caricatures of a tiny, slant-eyed half-people.

All were crystallized through Oppie's eyes and Phil's dilemma—the balance of one U.S. pilot against half a million Japanese citizens and visitors.

Should Phil have agreed to *not* warn targeted cities and their military installations? Most of the dissenting clergy, communists, Jews, political activists, and intellectuals had departed or, in the final solution, had been permanently silenced. Should not Hitler's master race—so white, so Christian, so Saxon, so German—have been bombed? At least the allied victors might have been spared the sight of Auschwitz, Dachau, and Bergen-Belsen, which still offends so many sensibilities.

Oppie and Groves were Nazi-haters certainly but residually respectful of Teutonic efficiency. Should not their neat plan for destroying two cities of black-eyed Asians have been overruled? Should they have announced a political demonstration, dropping the A-bomb in full official view off some South Pacific rim city? The most profound query remains, ignored and never answered: After Hiroshima, whatever could be Oppie's, Groves's, anyone's reason, three days later to drop a second bomb on Nagasaki?

The evolutionary theater and the ecological play, rather than the flashy onstage protagonists of the drama, are my concern. The answers are not simple, in part because the questions are not clearly phrased. The shadowed globe continues to spin. We are embedded in shared history, in all our personal histories. We are actors on the great stage of Earth's natural history from which there is no exit.

EPILOGUE

Photoblepharon

Más tira un pelito the Spaniards have been saying for centuries *que cien bueyes*: a pubic hair pulls more forcefully than a hundred oxen. The lure of science and knowledge is very strong but is often outmatched by the lure of pelitos. That human attractions for each other have enduring effects on the great course of scientific inquiry is perhaps underappreciated by readers of literature. Myriad original analyses and observations by hundreds of quietly obsessed scientists profoundly, if circuitously, influence the "civilized" world. But how does the private life of some obscure researcher alter public "progress" or inspire technological "revolution"? How might the sex life of the chief of medicine at the urban research hospital impede (or accelerate) the newest medical "miracle" that saves (or destroys) the reproductive organs of his young mistress . . . and of hundreds of other anonymously sterile women who are ready to pay?

How does the direct study of nature in nature, say of the night sky by an awkward and shy teenage astronomer, directly affect the probability of a lander to Mars and its return to Earth in 2025? Will the private dramas of two geologists—say, a petrologist and a geomorphologist—influence verification that magnetotactic bacteria, rod-shaped cells with tiny aligned magnets, were common inhabitants of our red, dusty, and today, entirely barren neighboring planet? Perhaps. Or maybe not. In this era where the majority of well-read, highly educated gentry ignore the wetness of nature to which we all owe our lives, the consequences are as numerous as they are obscure.

Perhaps my rude exposure of the personal side of real people (J. Robert Oppenheimer and Kitty, Phylis and Philip Morrison), as well as the fictional characters (Howard Fein, René Pemberlain Schiller, Raoul Gautier, Odile Bustamonte, Georges Standon, Mme. Denise LeClerc, and their colleagues), all of whom have little in common except passionate preoccupation with their own first-hand generation of scientific truth, helps answer these questions.

A small decision (say, whether to study Geology 101 or Chemistry 101 on Mondays and Wednesdays where the schedule has an opening) may have huge consequences to the future scientist. When a student elects chemistry, she is likely not to be aware of her invisible commitment to retorts, distillation apparatus, laboratory organics, heavy metals, weekends inside a deserted brick laboratory rather than field-work on the Triassic slopes of Mt. Sugarloaf or in the tin fields of Malaysia.

How do the textbooks, computer programs, or educational magazines obtain their "facts"? A paucity of dedicated loners generate the "scientific truths" that the rest of us accept on authority. The curious investigator himself fills up with doubt and self-criticism; when he reads the oversimplification or exaggeration attributed to him, he is usually embarrassed. He is dismayed by distortion of his work; he knows he never meant to contribute to problems of human health or environmental degradation. He knows in his heart of hearts what I know and what all my very best colleagues know: The continuous underlying international story of science may exist in some platonic sense, but it can never be told. Not only does no one even know the whole story from end to end but no one even *can* know it, in principle.

Glimpses accompany flashing insights. One fish at a time, *Photoblepharon* scintillates. The school reveals patchiness as the swarming swimmers expose their bacterial light in the dark waters of the Gulf of Aqaba. They illuminate and then darken the scuffling sediments below to provide an occasional glimpse. The dazzling flashes sparkle amidst the dullness of routine. I have modeled my prose after these denizens of the deep.

Nature, as we see, yields only with great reluctance and to very few who attempt to engage her. All spread of new knowledge is complicated by the lure of the pelitos and the warm, scented bait of the newborn. But science, in spite of its ignorant detractors, continues to spin its narrative, the big story of our natural history and the probable future of mankind. Potential young scientists and aged returnees in the scientific enterprise are not excluded, at least in principle, by the luck of their village of origin, the shape of their eyelids, or the hue of their skin.

"Science," as Stewart Brand says, "is the only news. Everything else is 'he said, she said.'" How, in spite of all diversions, selection pressures, and scarcities, science successfully describes a very few scenes illuminated by a very few fish is what I intend to bring to you. We remind each other that deep inside each flashlight fish, apparently without foresight or intention, when the density of trapped and healthily growing bacteria reaches some 10 million per teaspoon, the cold light abruptly turns on. The drab, now white-bellied fish becomes luminous to lead itself and its glow-in-the-dark symbionts to choice food and safe haven. Unplanned and unprayed-for nature just does it. And we are the beneficiaries.

ACKNOWLEDGMENTS

My greatest debt is to my literary and literal family: Jennifer Liff Margulis-di Properzio and James di Properzio, Ricardo Guerrero, Dorion Sagan, Jeremy Sagan, Zachary Margulis-Ohnuma, Tonio Sagan, Thomas N. Margulis, and Dennis Wepman, all of whom have, to varying degrees since 1978, helped with this long-incubating manuscript.

I also thank my father, Morris Alexander, and my colleagues who are (or were) also friends: Edward Tripp, G. Evelyn Hutchinson, Ernst Mayr, Elso S. Barghoorn (paleontologist), Claude Monty (sedimentologist), Roger Chesselet (oceanographer), Lewis Thomas (medical scientist and poet), Philip (astonomer) and Phylis (educator) Morrison, Ernest (Chick) Callenbach (writer), Kameshwar Wali (physicist), Antonio Lazcano (biologist), Kenneth Nealson (microbiologist), James Lovelock (atmospheric chemist), and Sir David C. Smith (symbiosis biologist). Unfortunately the first nine in this list did not live to see the work completed. Lewis Lapham, Michelle Presse, William Frucht, and Janet Williams (editors) were serious critics. So did Peter Westbroek (paleontologist), Wolfi Krumbein (geomicrobiologist), biologists Anna Gorbushina, David Bermudes, Michael Chapman, Michael Dolan, Mercé Piqueras, Margaret McFall-Ngai, Ned Ruby, Marie-Odile Soyer-Gobillard, Gunther Stent, and J. Woody Hastings, and publishers Klaus and Alice Peters (A. K. Publishers, Natick, MA).

Hard criticism from friends coupled with many painful editors' rejections helped shape the work. This includes comments and aid from Celeste Asikainen, Dianne Bilyak, Lois Brynes, Kirk Jenson, and Barbara Riddle. Subtlety is not approved in the writing of professional scientific articles where one can never describe experience too explicitly. Thus all my previous training conspired to lead me in the opposite direction from this sort of literary expression. Although D. Ehhalt, P.-P. Grassé, André Hollande, H. D. Holland, William Kellogg, Philip Morrison, J. R. Oppenheimer, S. Ramón y Cajal and Carl Sagan are (or were) scientists, all others and their stories are my plausible inventions. Judith Herrick Beard (TYPRO), Joan Howard Gross, and Donna Reppard have been superb and patient typists throughout the years. Judy Beard caught and corrected a slew of last-minute errors and oversights. So did the competent editors at my beloved publisher, Chelsea Green Publishing Company: John Barstow, Bill Bokermann, Jonathan Teller-Elsberg, Jim Wallace, Margo and Ian Baldwin. The Lounsbery Foundation, Marta Norman, the University of Massachusetts, The Tauber Fund, Abraham Gomel of Liberté dairy products in Candiac, Quebec, the Rockefeller Foundation at Bellagio, Italy, receipt of the marvelous prize from the Alexander von Humboldt Stiftung, and grants from NASA all helped with financial support, if inadvertently. That Tusquets (Miguel Aguilar, Jorge Wagensberg, Toni Lopez, Juan Cerezo, and Beatriz diMaura) agreed to Spanish language publication long before this work saw the light of day in my native language, delights me still. That my new agent, Georges Borchardt in 2004 accepted the manuscript marked the end of rejections in my mind. I am eternally grateful to him. The hospitality of the Hanse Wissenschaftskolleg (Delmenhorst, Germany) and its director Gerhard Roth permitted completion of this work.

Please see reference to our scientific work on *www.science writers.org*, most of which attempts with great difficulty not to be fiction.